Miss Janet, Peplow

9, waterworks Road,

Barbourne,

Worcester.

Janet Sybil Irene Peplow

age 11 years.

(27)

The escape from the bull.

GEORGIE MERTON

FLORENCE HARRINGTON

THOMAS NELSON AND SONS, LTD.

LONDON, EDINBURGH, AND NEW YORK

PRINTED IN GREAT BRITAIN AT
THE PRESS OF THE PUBLISHERS.

CONTENTS.

LIST OF ILLUSTRATIONS.

GEORGIE MERTON.

CHAPTER I.

THE SPILT INKSTAND.

T was a day in the changeful month of April,
and a real April day; for though the sun
would show its face perhaps ten minutes at
a time, the heavy showers were certain to
come down, and people who were able were
only too glad to stay indoors. Thus it was that the
room known as the school-room at Merton House
was such a scene of merriment. It was the play-
hour. Their gentle governess had disappeared, and
so the children could give full vent to their romping
spirits. Georgie was seated cross-legged on the
centre of the table, notwithstanding the dangerous
proximity of a well-filled inkstand, and was just
now engaged in dragging up her twin-brother Conrad
to share her elevated position.

"Tom, will you leave off pulling Con's leg? you are hurting him. I will tell mother, if you don't. Now, Con, my man, give a spring, and up you are! Hurrah!" she cried, as her delicate-looking, pale-faced little brother succeeded in scrambling to her side. "Now you and I, Con, will be able to keep those two young ones off. This is our castle, and won't we just fight?"

Tom, a small boy of seven, then rushed up to the table, followed by Cyril, usually called Twig—the baby of the family, who was only four years old, and very tiny for his age — and armed with long sticks, formed of brown paper rolled up tightly, they made a desperate attack, but were beaten off with weapons of the same description. The game had now become so exciting that Alice—the book-worm, and in general a most properly-behaved young lady of about fourteen—came out of her corner, and, putting down her book, was in a few seconds as busily engaged as the rest, whilst the shouts of laughter became louder every moment.

Just, however, as the garrison was beginning to grow rather exhausted by so much exertion, the door suddenly opened with a creak; and Georgie, shifting her position to see who was entering, upset the table, and down the twins, lesson-books, and inkstand went with a crash upon the floor! The frightened children screamed frantically; but Georgie was up in a minute, and busily engaged in extricating Con, whilst the new-comer exclaimed:

"Oh, you children, you children! you always are up to mischief. It is lucky for you that it was me, and not Miss Acton, who came in."

"Do you suppose I care for either her or you one atom, Miss Lily?" cried Georgie, trying to wipe the ink off the poor ill-used carpet with her pocket-handkerchief.

"Georgie, do stop," said Lily, laughing: "just come here." And having dragged her to a small looking-glass hanging on one of the walls—"Look at yourself," she said; "only just look at yourself! Did you ever see such a sweet creature?"

Poor Georgie! it was not often she was shame-faced, or she certainly would have been now, with her face all stained with ink, hands, dress, and shaggy mane splashed, and her brothers and sisters all laughing at her.

"Well, I don't care.—Just let me see, Con, if you are safe. Oh, that's right; you haven't a speck on you.—I can't help it, Lily; I am always in scrapes. But I don't care."

"'Don't care' came to the gallows; mind you don't," sung out Tom.

" Hold your tongue, Tom, and hand us your hand-kerchief.—There now, Lily ; is not that cleanly done? The carpet looks only a few shades darker; I declare I think it is an improvement.—Here, Alice, you finish off tidying, and see the books are all out. It is only five minutes to lesson-time, and I must go and wash myself."

The next minute Georgie was bounding up the stairs two steps at a time ; and having landed safely in the room she shared with Alice, she commenced scrubbing her face vigorously with quantities of soap, and washing out the stains on her dress. She had not a quarter finished when the bell rang for lessons ; but she rapidly dashed the towel over her face and the front of her dress, and hurried down-stairs to be in time.

Miss Acton was already in the school-room. She was a gentle woman, and always wore a melancholy, resigned look, as if she had known much trouble. She was not a favourite with the children ; though they would have been at a loss to define what it was they disliked in her. Perhaps it was that she was wanting in life, and went through her daily routine of work in a manner too much like a machine. Georgie entered quietly, for her, and hoped to escape notice ; but at that moment the sun shone out brightly, and her stained face, wet hair, and unfortunate dress could not be hid.

"Oh, Georgie, what have you been doing? What a dreadful condition you are in!"

"I am really very sorry, Miss Acton; but—but we were playing at castles, and I fell off the table and threw down the inkstand. I washed my face well with soap; and my frock is not my best one."

"Georgie, my dear, you have disobeyed me again about getting on the table; and Mrs. Merton said next time you did so, I must tell her. I am very sorry. But now run upstairs, and get nurse to put you tidy, and then come and begin your afternoon work."

Lessons went on pretty smoothly now, and without any particular interruption. As soon as they were over—which was at a quarter to six, school-room tea being at six o'clock—Miss Acton said: "Now, Georgie, you must stay here, whilst I go to speak to Mrs. Merton. I am really very sorry to have to complain to her; and this is the third time within the last fortnight."

Georgie did not seem to feel as much as the governess the weight of her sin. Anyhow, at that moment, with her arm round Con's neck, Twig holding on to her skirts, and a merry smile on her face, she did not look much depressed.

We will follow Miss Acton into the drawing-room, where Mrs. Merton was sitting, a book open on her knees, but not apparently engaged in reading, as her eyes were closed, and at first the governess thought she slept. She was a woman with a calm, tranquil expression; her hair was slightly tinged with gray; her age about forty. She turned her head as Miss Acton was going to withdraw, and with a sweet smile said, in a kind, genial voice:

"Is that you, Miss Acton? Don't go away; I am not asleep, only idle. You look tired; come and sit down in this low chair and have a chat. I hope the children have not been extra troublesome."

"Thanks, Mrs. Merton; I cannot stay—tea will be ready in a few minutes. The children have all been good enough at their lessons; but I am sorry to tell you that Georgie has disobeyed me again about getting on the table during play-time. She did so this afternoon; and she and the table came down together, and of course the inkstand which is kept on it. I fear her dress is utterly spoiled."

A grave, anxious expression came over Mrs. Merton's face, and she waited a second before she answered:
"I am really much distressed to hear of this. Poor Georgie seems always to be in trouble; but she must learn to obey. I won't detain you longer now, Miss

Acton; but after tea will you kindly send Georgie to my dressing-room?"

Half an hour later Georgie, with her arm round Conrad as usual, appeared in the dressing-room.

" Conrad, dear, you must not stay here now; you must go back to the school-room. I want to speak to Georgie alone for a few minutes."

" Yes, I know, mother; but I was just as naughty as Geo, for I got on the table too."

" O Con, you never told me you were going to tell mother that.—Indeed, mother, it was all my fault for I made him come up, and it was I upset the table."

" Con, were you ever told not to get on the table?"

" No, mother; but Georgie was, so I thought I must not get on too."

" Well then, dear boy, as you were not told not to, you did not disobey, and I can let you off; but remember for the future you must never do so. And now give me a kiss and go at once."

The little fellow,—he was twelve, though no one would have taken him for nine or ten, so small and delicate-looking was he,—dared linger no longer. He threw his arms round his mother's neck, kissed her fondly, and casting a pitying glance at Georgie, whispered in her ear, " Don't scold her too much," and left the room.

As soon as the door was closed, Georgie went up closer to her mother, and looking in her face said gravely, "I don't know how it is, mother, for I am sure I do try to be better, but somehow I forget, and then 'tis so exciting. I wish I could be like Lily, though I know I never shall. She never gets into scrapes, and I don't think I am ever out of them;" and then she placed her hands behind her back, and put on a very comical expression of distress.

"My dearest child, it is all very well to talk thus, but you really must try to put some restraint on yourself, and learn to obey when you are spoken to. This is the third time within the last fortnight that I have had occasion to speak to you, and you cannot think how grieved I am to find my Georgie makes no effort to improve herself."

Mrs. Merton spoke very earnestly; and Georgie, with her eyes cast down, said in a low voice, "I am very sorry, mother, but I believe I am beyond improving. I am awfully wicked, I know."

"Indeed I trust you are nothing of the kind, Georgie; but something must be done to make you better than you are. Father thinks the same as I do, for I have been talking to him about it; he does not at all like a disobedient little daughter."

"O mother, you have not told father, have you?

What shall I do? he does so hate for me to be naughty," said poor Georgie, bursting into a flood of tears, and hiding her face in her mother's lap.

"Yes, I have, my darling. I wanted his advice; and this is what he and I think—that it will be best for our little girl to stay at home next Saturday when the others go to Mure Hill. It will be a great disappointment to you, my child, I know, but you have brought your punishment on yourself. I trust such a thing will never happen again."

Georgie sobbed bitterly for some minutes, for she knew very well that what her mother said was true, and that it was entirely her own fault that had brought it on her. At last she looked up, and when she saw the tears stealing down Mrs. Merton's cheeks, she choked her sobs and said, "Don't cry, mother darling, please don't; I am not worth crying about. I really will try to be a good girl. I know it's all my own wicked heart."

Her mother said nothing, but, drawing her close, kissed her many times, and sent her back to the school-room just as the gong sounded for dinner.

Georgie entered with a very subdued expression, and the tears still rolling down her cheeks. Miss Acton, having given her a hasty glance, continued her knitting; but Conrad seized hold of his sister and pulled her down into a comfortable corner, whither the others soon followed; even Alice left her books, and Twig his bricks, to try to comfort poor Georgie.

"What did mother say, Geo? is she very angry?" asked Alice.

"Don't cry any more, there's a jolly old girl," whispered Tom; whilst baby Twiggie lisped out, "Me will wipe your eyes, Deo, and dive you my lubly new top."

Georgie cried on a few minutes, and then laughing through her tears at her group of comforters, said, "Well, I do believe I am the most unfortunate girl that ever lived! Of course 'tis all my own fault, I know, but father and mother say I am not to go to Mure Hill on Saturday."

There was a general groan at this announcement and then one and all said, almost at the same moment, "I hope 'twill rain, then! We shan't enjoy ourselves a bit without you."

"No, no, don't be geese," said Georgie; "I hope 'twill be fine; and then if I can only manage to keep good, I can go next time.—Give me a kiss, Twig, my duckie, for here's nurse come to march you off to bed, and I must learn my lessons for to-morrow. Come on, Con, help me up, and see if I don't learn my lessons quicker than you to-night."

CHAPTER II.

THE FALSE ALARM.

URE HILL was the residence of Miss Merton, the children's only aunt, a charming old lady, many years older than her brother, devoted to her nephews and nieces, and a day spent with her was always esteemed the greatest of treats from the eldest to the youngest. Consequently, not to be allowed to visit her was regarded as the severest punishment, especially as Aunt Margaret always insisted upon knowing the reason of the banishment.

Saturday came round at last, and every one was up early so as to start directly breakfast was ended. The children were going first, under charge of Miss Acton and old nurse; and as the distance was about four miles, Alice and Conrad rode their ponies, whilst the donkey-cart was put in requisition for the others, Tom acting as coachman. Mr. and Mrs. Merton, with Norman and Lily, their eldest son and

daughter, were coming over later in the day. Poor
Georgie, she bore up bravely, assisted in getting
every one off, and then, having had a good cry and
made no end of resolutions as to her future conduct,
she wandered about the garden until one of the
house-maids came to tell her that her dinner was
ready. She did not care for the solitary meal,
though cook, taking pity on her, sent up some of
her favourite dishes. A few minutes sufficed to
satisfy her hunger, and then she settled down to
prepare her lessons for the next day.

Meanwhile, the party at Mure Hill were enjoying
themselves immensely, though every now and then
thoughts of the culprit at home would come into
their minds, and shadows would flit across the happy
faces. Miss Merton was very sorry not to have
Georgie, as, with all her noisy, tomboyish ways, she
was a great favourite with the old lady. Con, too,
wanted her many times. She was his protector,
being much taller and stronger than he was: in fact,
Connie was much more fitted, with his timid, gentle
ways, to be a girl than was his high-spirited sister.

The morning was spent in running and racing all
over the place, visiting the farm-yard, seeing the
baby pigs, and all those other treasures of the
farmer's wife which children so dearly love. Nurse

went to have a gossip with the old house-keeper, her special friend; and Miss Acton went off alone to a picturesque spot about quarter of a mile distant to complete an unfinished sketch. Aunt Margaret thus had her children to herself, and very contented did she seem, though they dragged her here and there, and would all talk together. At length the hour came for dinner, and back to the house they went, just in time to welcome Mr. and Mrs. Merton, Norman and Lily, as they alighted from the carriage.

Dinner at Mure Hill was always a treat to the children. Miss Merton's old house-keeper knew what each liked best, and had no end of goodies in readiness for such occasions; to which they well knew how to do justice.

After dinner the elders retired to the drawing-room for a chat; Twig was handed over to nurse's care; Miss Acton hurried off to put the last few touches to her sketch; and the rest of the party, under the charge of Norman and Lily, departed for what they called a scramble. Presently they reached a small wood that lay near the house, and here they set to work to amuse themselves. Alice and Con began to gather violets. Lily sometimes assisted them, and sometimes wandered off alone to discover some more lovely spot where finer specimens were to

be found.   Tom amused himself with climbing trees;
Norman with watching the antics of his young
brother. Suddenly all were startled by a loud cry
from Lily:—

"Norman! Norman!—Alice! come here—quick!
Look what I have found!"

The wood lay on the side of a hill, and Lily had
just come upon one of those great fissures which are
often to be discovered in rocky districts.

"Did you ever see anything so delightful? Isn't
it a splendid place? Fancy our never finding it out
before!"

The others were charmed. The gloom which
enveloped it, and the excitement of the discovery,
so overcame them, that a plan was instantly set on
foot to explore this wonderful place, and see where it
led to.

"Who knows what extraordinary things we may
come upon," said Alice.

"I wish Geo were here; how wild she would be,
dear old Geo," said Lily.—"But come, Norman, who is
to be leader, you or I?"

"Oh, I will, of course," said her brother, a fine,
handsome young fellow, who was now reading with
a clergyman near his home, previous to his going up
to Oxford. He was the eldest of the family, and

eighteen years of age, and his parents were justly proud of their first-born son, who was endowed with many gifts, both of mind and body, and had beyond a few childish faults, notwithstanding his haughty, high-spirited temperament, given them no anxiety since his birth. Lily was next to him in age, and was in every way a sweet, amiable girl, her mother's right hand, and her father's pet. Scarlet fever had carried off two boys, who came between her and Alice, which accounted for the difference in age between them.

The party now entered the cavern; poor Con, though trembling, making up his mind to be brave for Georgie's sake; and Tom, rejoicing in the novelty of the place, making the walls re-echo with his merry shouts,—

"Go on quicker, Norman!—Don't lag behind, you girls!—Connie, you are a muff! I believe you are half afraid!—Now this is what I call, just jolly."

The cavern was very lofty, and at first it was no difficult matter to advance through the twilight; but at last it became so dark that Norman, who was in front, came back and said to Lily,—

"Do you know, I don't think we should go any further in this darkness. One cannot tell what kind of place this may be, so really it is not safe."

"Very well, if you think it best, we will go back;

though I must confess I should like to find out where
it leads to. Perhaps auntie will be able to tell us
something about it. If we could only—"

A wild shriek interrupted Lily, and, turning quickly
round, she saw Tom running with all his speed, and
Alice dragging Con as fast as she could go, both
screaming, to the entrance of the cavern. She and
Norman were soon with them, inquiring what was
the matter. Alice answered first,—

"Oh, it was a horrible thing came in our faces. O
Lily, do come home!"

Con looked on the verge of fainting, and was
shaking and trembling from head to foot. Norman
sat down on a large stone close by, and, taking the
frightened child in his arms, did his best to comfort
him.

"Be a man, Con; why, 'twas only a poor bat, that
would not hurt any one. That is its bed-room in
there: it always sleeps in the day-time, and all of
us noisy folks coming in disturbed it. You are all
right now, aren't you? What will Georgie say?
Come, cheer up, and be a brave boy, and we will go
back and tell auntie and father and mother all
about our grand discovery, shall we?—Come on,
girls, it is time we started homewards.—Hollo!
where's that monkey Tom? surely I saw him running

out." Then, turning to Alice, he added, "You weren't afraid too, were you, Alice? Was it not last week I heard you delivering a lecture on bats in the school-room?"

"Oh no, Norman, I was not in the least frightened for myself, but only for Connie. Of course, I am not afraid of harmless little creatures like bats."

Now this was not quite true, for it was only a few minutes before that Alice had called the bat "a horrible thing." But the broad light of day had restored her presence of mind, and she would not condescend to own that she had been in the least disturbed.

The party now wended their way towards Mure Hill, shouting at intervals for Tom (though Lily declared she felt almost sure he must have run home), and stopping every now and then to increase their store of violets. Just at the end of the wood they came upon Mr. Merton, his wife, sister, and three or four servants, all looking very anxious, and the missing Tom just a little in advance of them, as if acting as guide. When the two parties came in sight of each other, Mr. Merton stood still, cast a hasty glance towards the young people, and then, exclaiming, "Thank God, they are all safe!" rushed forward, and clasped the astonished Con to his breast. Norman could not at all understand this proceeding, and as soon as they were come up to each other, every one began asking questions, and the elders to express a good deal of thankfulness.

"But, father, mother, auntie, what do you mean?" exclaimed the violet gatherers; "we have not been in any danger, we have only been here in the wood."

"But the horrible dark place, with the animals!" said Mr. Merton.

"The creature that tried to eat up my precious boy!" added Mrs. Merton.

"The awful sounds, and the black things in the air!" cried Miss Merton.

Norman could not repress a smile as he answered quickly, "Please don't be alarmed. The only place we have been to which at all answers this description, is an old cavern in the side of yonder hill, into which we went, and advanced some little way, until it became too dark to see; and just as we turned to go out, a poor bat, whose slumbers we had disturbed, flew into Con's face, and rather frightened him. That is all, I can assure you."

"The old cavern," repeated Miss Merton—"the old cavern. Do you mean one with the entrance much covered up with shrubs and bushes? Why, Henry"— and she placed her hand on her brother's arm—"don't you recollect it? Why, we used to play there as children. But I thought the entrance was so completely overgrown now, that no one could find it."

"It was I made the discovery, Aunt Margaret," said Lily. "I was never more surprised, for I vainly imagined I knew every bit of this wood thoroughly. But where does it lead to, and why did you never tell us of its existence?"

"I don't know, my dear, how large it is, or where it leads to. Your father and I used often to play there, but we never ventured very far in. And I never told you that there was such a place, for the simple reason that I had forgotten it. Why, I don't think I have set foot in there for fifty years. Isn't it quite as long as that, Henry?"

"Mother," interrupted Alice, "who told you we were in such a terrible place? Surely it was not Tom."

"Indeed it was, my dear Alice. Your father had gone round to the stables, and your aunt and I were sitting working in the drawing-room, when the door was thrown open, and Tom rushed in, in such a state of excitement and fright that we were quite terrified. We could at first scarcely understand what he said but anyhow he so alarmed us about all of you, that we instantly called your father and some of the servants, and started off at once to the rescue, wondering, indeed, if you were still alive."

"Little coward," muttered Norman under his breath; whilst aloud he added, "Where is he gone to now? It is really too bad of him to be so silly. Why, he was wild to go on further, until Con cried out when the bat flew in his face; and then he took to his heels as fast as if twenty hob-goblins had been after him.—Here, Tom, Tom, Tommie, where are you gone to? Come here, we want you! Tom, do you hear?"

It was in vain he called; no Tom answered him. They had by this time reached the house, where tea was awaiting them. The gong sounded, but no Tom came; and at last when the carriage, the donkey-cart, and the ponies had been brought round, and every one was ready and waiting to set off on the journey homewards, Norman, who had been searching all over the house, the gardens, and the farm-yard in vain, betook himself to the stables, as being the last place where he could be hidden. His search was as fruitless here as elsewhere, and he was returning to the house with a wearied expression on his face, when the kitchen-maid suddenly appeared, and dropping him a low courtesy, said,—

"Please, Mr. Norman, Jane told me as you were

looking for little Master Tom. I saw him myself, about half an hour ago, running down the lane which leads to Mr. Morris's mill. I thought as you would excuse my telling you, sir;" and dropping another courtesy, the girl went back to her own regions. Norman hurried up to his father, who was standing on the door-step, looking rather annoyed, as he well might, at this long delay, and said hastily,—

"I have not found him yet, father, but I have just heard where he is, and will bring him back in a few minutes."

Without waiting for a reply he darted off again, and in a very short space of time reached the mill. At the door of the miller's house stood fat Mrs. Morris, as good-natured a woman as ever lived, and always a favourite with children, to whom, having none of her own, she was most devoted.

"Well, Master Norman, and how be you now? It's many a long day since I've seen you; and what a big young gentleman you are growing, to be sure."

"I am all right, thanks, Mrs. Morris. I have come down to hunt up that young brother of mine, Tom. Have you seen him this afternoon?"

"Sure now, Master Norman, I saw him not twenty minutes agone go into the room where the fresh flour is kept. He said he wanted something, I scarce know what, he seemed in such a hurry like, and rushed by me hardly without speaking."

"Oh, you will excuse me, Mrs. Morris, I am certain," answered Norman. "My father and all the others are waiting to go home; but we can't find this young monkey, and we can't set off till we have found him." And so saying, he hastened to the room she had pointed out. Entering, he saw only a number of great sacks and casks of flour; and having walked round calling "Tom," he was just about to leave the apartment, when a sound,—could it be his fancy?—somewhat like a suppressed sob, met his ear. He paused and listened; surely he was not mistaken, there it was again.

"Tom," he called out, "is that you? Where are you?" and he gazed round the apparently vacant room in vain, not a vestige of anything like the truant was to be seen. But now the sobs became louder, and a faint voice said,—

"Norman, O dear Norman, do come and help me out!"

Norman stood still a moment in amazement; that was certainly Tom's voice speaking out of the great cask opposite him, and he hastily crossed the room to it. It was a very large cask, and happened to be placed on the top of two small ones, so that do his utmost, and stand on the very tips of his toes, Norman could not look inside it; so he climbed up, and, with one foot resting on one of the smaller casks, peered within. The next instant he was down again; and tired and worried though he was with his long search, he could not refrain from giving way to a merry peal of laughter.

"Oh, oh! Tom, I can't help it, indeed I can't!" as the little fellow began to howl piteously; "but to see you there it is enough to upset any one! However, we must get you out somehow. How in the world you ever got in, I can't imagine. Now, stop bellowing, and see what we can do. Father and all have been waiting an age. Stand up; that's right. Now see, I will stand on this lower cask,—it is lucky I have my old clothes on,—put your arms round my neck, and see if you can't drag yourself up."

A little tugging, and a few slips, and then Norman landed himself on the floor with his burden on his back.

"A nice sort of boy you are!—Steady; now, you may as well keep quiet, for I don't intend to let you go again, so please be content to remain where you are. O Tommie, what will become of you, if, at your tender age, you take to hiding in flour-casks?"

With Norman laughing, and poor Tom sobbing out at intervals, "Oh, what will they say?" the pair at last reached the party gathered in front of Mure Hill House. Norman began running as soon as he came in sight of them; and before they could recover their surprise, Tom stood in their midst. All eyes rested on him, and a very extraordinary and pitiful object did he look. He was well floured over from the crown of his head to the soles of his feet; and his tears had been so many, that there were regular little gutters down his cheeks where they had rolled. At first no one could resist the temptation to laugh.

"Tom is a drate white man now, fader! Poor Tom, s'all I do and tiss him, fader?" lisped out Twiggie. At length, Norman having explained where he had found him, Mr. Merton asked Tom how he came to be in such a place. Between his sobs the runaway gasped out,—

"I wanted to hide, be-because I thought you would be angry be-because I frightened you about Con—oh! oh! I thought it was an empty, emp-ty c-a-s-k,— oh! indeed I did,—oh! oh! oh!" and he roared in the most dreadful manner.

"You are a very silly, cowardly, naughty little boy," said his father, "and we all feel thoroughly ashamed of you. Now cease that noise at once, and go and get into the back of the donkey-cart. You must sit by yourself, or you will flour every one else.—Miss Acton, I daresay you won't mind driving old Jack home.—Good-bye, dear Margaret. I hope next time I bring you such a party over, that there will not be so many catastrophes. We really must hurry home, it is so late."

The good-byes were over at last, and the Merton family fairly started on their way homewards. The journey was a pleasant one, for the elders had much to talk about, and the young ones were full of the day's adventures—and how much there was to tell Georgie! Twig was the only quiet one, for he fell asleep soon after they started. As to Tom, he lay all in a heap at the bottom of the cart, feeling heartily ashamed of himself, and inclined to be very sulky in consequence But this he was not allowed to be, as Alice and Con kept their ponies close; and after a little coaxing and persuading, drew forth from him a full account of how he had come to think of hiding in the flour-cask, how he had felt when there, and his great joy at hearing Norman's voice, though he was afraid to call out at first. In fact he had quite made up his mind that he should be left there all night, for he had made many frantic efforts, but in vain, to get out of his prison.

" My face feels so stiff," said he at last, " as if it were all stuck together."

At this the others laughed, and Alice suggested that water and flour made paste; so, of course, his tears had made paste on his cheeks. At this Tom felt much inclined to make some more paste, but he changed his mind, and laughed instead, whilst nurse called out to him,—

" You may expect a good scrubbing in your bath to-night, Master Tom; I believe I shall have to use a scrubbing-brush to get you clean."

CHAPTER III.

NE afternoon a few days after the expedition to Mure Hill, lessons being over, the children were all summoned downstairs into their mother's presence. Mrs. Merton was working when they entered the room, but at once put her work down, and regarded the group before her with rather a grave expression on her face. Alice had a book under her arm; Tom stood next her, with both hands in his knickerbocker pockets; Georgie had Twig on her back, his pretty curly head peeping at his mother over her shoulder; and Con had his hand resting on her arm.

"My dear children, I sent for you as I wanted to ask if either of you could tell me anything about this old china vase. It is one your father values very much, and this morning I discovered that it was broken. I have already questioned the servants and your elder brother and sisters; but they know nothing at all about it. Hester says she is certain it was not broken when she dusted the room, so it must have been done since. Now, think before you answer, and if either of you has been so unfortunate as to break it, don't be afraid to tell the truth."

Mrs. Merton stopped speaking, and the children all declared they knew nothing of it, and were preparing to leave the room, when Mrs. Merton called them back, and said gently,—

"Don't think I doubt your word, for I cannot believe that either of you would tell me a deliberate falsehood, but still I would like to ask each of you separately.—Alice, was it you?"

"No, mother; I have not been in here to-day."

"Georgie, was it you?"

"Oh no, mother!" gasped Georgie, for Twig was pulling her hair.

"Not me, mother," put in the little tormentor.

"I did not break it," added Tom.

"Did you, Conrad?"

"No, mother," was again the answer; and then they all departed to make ready for their walk.

"It is a very extraordinary thing, dear Henry," said Mrs. Merton, half an hour later to her husband, "but I can find out nothing about that vase. I have questioned both children and servants, and they deny all knowledge of it. I cannot make out the matter at all, as Hester persists that it was not broken when she dusted the room this morning."

"Well, the thing is provoking, certainly. Hester is a trusty girl. Did you ask all the children—that monkey Tom as well as the rest?"

"Yes, dear, twice over; and each time they all gave the same answer."

Nothing more was said on the subject, and it was allowed to drop.

That afternoon was a memorable one in the history of the Merton family. Miss Acton and her charges returned home about three-quarters of an hour before lessons commenced; for as the sky began to be over-clouded, she very rightly deemed that it would be safer for her pupils in this treacherous spring weather to be nearer home. They had scarcely reached the house, however, before the sky grew blue overhead, the sun shone forth, and everything without looked so delightful, that Georgie and the boys begged to be allowed to spend the half hour of freedom that still remained to them in searching for forget-me-nots by the pond in the lower meadow. Alice preferred remaining indoors; she was just in the most interesting part of a story-book Aunt Margaret had lent her.

After some little persuasion, Miss Acton gave the desired permission; adding an injunction, however, that on no account was Georgie to climb any trees, as she had on her tidy frock, and they were to be sure to come back directly they heard the five o'clock bell ring.

Having promised to do this, off started the trio in high spirits. On their way down the drive they met nurse coming back from her walk with Twig. The little fellow ran to meet them, and two minutes after was perched on Georgie's back, his loving arms clasped tightly round her neck.

"Where is you doing to? I wants to tum too. Do take me, dearie Deo; I'll be tuch a dood boy."

"All right, my sonnie. Hold on tight, and I will ask nurse." Off she rushed. "Nurse, nurse! we are going down to the lower pond to get forget-me-nots; may we take Twig? Mother let us take him last time;—we will take care he does not get into the water."

"Me wants to do so much, nursie. P'ease let me do."

"Very well, my pet;—but now mind, Miss Georgie, you take care of him. And now be off all of you, or the bell will ring before you are down there."

Nurse continued her way to the house and in a

very short space of time the party reached the pond, and were busily engaged in gathering the forget-me-nots which grew there in great profusion. Very soon they had each gathered a capital nosegay of the "little blue-eyes," as Twiggie always persisted in calling them. Suddenly a cry from Tom, who was about a hundred yards off, was heard, and, turning quickly round, the children perceived him running towards them looking dreadfully scared. In a few seconds they knew the reason as he shouted, " Farmer Hill's black bull has broken loose and is galloping towards us ! "

Georgie thought for one instant, and then her resolution was taken. This bull was a very furious one, and was generally kept locked up, as he had tossed several people already; so there was no play about the matter, but real danger.

" We must get up into the oak tree," said she; and snatching up Twig in her arms, she ran, or rather flew, over the ground to a tree about twenty paces distant, screaming to the other two to follow her. In less time than it takes to describe it, she had reached the tree. It was one of those very old ones whose trunks measure yards round, and whose branches grow close to the ground. Often had the children climbed it for pleasure.

The roaring of the bull sounded quite close now; a few moments more and he would be on them, and then—but Georgie did not wait to think about that, she acted. Up, Con, up!" she cried; and putting Twig down for a second, she gave him a helping hand. "Now you are up, that's right. Quick now; put one hand round that branch, and drag up Twig with the other. That's it. Hold tight, my sonnie! Put your foot on that knob. Are you safe?—Now, Tom, there's not an instant to spare. Hollo! Now give a spring and up you are. Now, lend me your hand,—the brute will be here in a second." And Georgie, having thus provided for the safety of her brothers, commenced her own ascent. She was half way up, and had only to put her foot into the hole in the bark, and put up her hands to catch hold of the bough, when the infuriated animal reached the tree, and the brave girl could feel his steaming breath! She made a frantic effort. Many and many a time had she climbed this tree—she was reckoned more sure-footed than the boys—yet now at this supreme moment her foot slipped! A wild shriek rose from the boys, for the bull was there beneath the bough. Con hid his face in his hands, afraid to look; Tom, knowing he could do no good, held Twig tightly and gazed down in breathless anxiety. Georgie fell, but

how was it she did not fall far? The bull was
savagely pawing the ground beneath the part where
she was, and marvellous to relate, she so fell that she
alighted on his back! This was how it was that she
did not reach the earth. Even now her presence of
mind did not forsake her. Life is very precious, and
Georgie determined not to sell hers without making
every effort to save it. She grabbed hold of the
animal's hair. What was that her hand came upon?
Tight round his neck was wound the piece of rope
that had served as his halter. Immediately she
seized upon it with both hands. The animal felt the
sudden weight upon his back, he lifted his head,
uttered a prodigious roar, kicked up his hind legs,
and once more started off on his mad career.

Now was the time of peril for poor Georgie. The
bull's back was a broad one; she could ride a horse
at full gallop, but her present steed was a much more
difficult one to manage. However, she held on
frantically and with her utmost strength, at the same
time offering a prayer to her Father in heaven that
he would save her in this hour of danger.

On tore the enraged animal over the meadow as
hard as his unwieldy body could go. He could
not make out the burden on his back. Once he
stopped and kicked furiously and tore up the grass

with his horns. Georgie trembled lest he should take to rolling, for then she knew nothing less than a miracle could save her.

"O God, do have mercy on me! Do send some one to save me!" she cried.

Again the bull went on. Her strength was well-nigh gone, her wrists seemed as if they must break off, when surely she could not be mistaken, she heard voices shouting. Yes, that was father's voice; help was coming! The bull seemed to hear the sounds too, for he suddenly stood still, and turning straight round, rushed in the direction from whence they proceeded. A minute more and he was arrested by several pitch-forks, held towards him by some of Farmer Hill's stalwart labourers. He burst through them, though the blood trickled down his hide, and made his way to a hedge, endeavouring to jump over it. He missed his footing and fell into the ditch. The men hastened up.

"My child! my child!" cried the unhappy father.

The bull scrambled to his feet again; but Georgie, where was she? She was no longer on his back!

"Georgie, my child, my child!" again arose the agonizing cry, for the little girl was nowhere to be seen.

"Here she be, please your honour," shouted out

one of the men, who had been examining the ditch a few yards higher up.

Mr. Merton hurried to the spot, and the next minute the labourer had lifted Georgie up and placed her, apparently lifeless, in her father's arms.

"She is not gone, sir; see, the colour is coming back," said the man, as he sprinkled her face with cooling water.

"No, she is not," said Mr. Merton. "I must take her home; and, Hill, just see that that beast is properly secured, or he will be doing some more damage. He really ought to be shot."

"Yes, sir, and that he shall be, though he is worth a goodish deal of money, before ever this night's over."

They had now reached the end of the meadow, and bidding the men go after the bull, Mr. Merton hurriedly walked up to his house, and but a short time elapsed before Georgie was undressed and lying in her own little bed. She was conscious, though she could not speak; and when the old doctor came presently, he said she had broken no bones, but had sprained her ankle very badly, and her whole system had received a severe shock, from which she might not recover for several weeks. He then ordered her to be given a soothing draught, to have cold pads put on her head and ankle, and to be kept as quiet as possible. Here we will leave her for the present, looking very pale, with closed eyes, and her mother and eldest sister bending over her, speaking cheering words, and every now and then changing her pads, whilst we go back a while to see what has become of the boys we left perched in the great oak tree. Tom induced Con to look up, when he perceived his courageous sister start off on her dangerous ride.

"O Tom, Tom, she will be killed!" he cried out in horror. "O Georgie! Dear Geo!"

"Dod will take tare of dear Deo," sobbed out Twig, who was crying bitterly. "Ask Him, Tonnie; mother said He would. I fordet my p'ayers now."

"You are right, darling Twiggie," said his brother, down whose cheeks the tears were also streaming. "But oh, do look at the brute! She will be off, she will be off!"

"Say p'ayers, Tom; oh, do say p'ayers, Tonnie!"

"I can't, Twig; I'm too wicked," cried Con. "Do you, Tom, before it is too late. Oh, my darling Georgie! what shall I do if you are killed?" and the boy's whole frame shook so much with the violence of his sobs, that Tom had to snatch hold of his arm to prevent his falling off the bough he was seated upon.

"Will Dod hear a little p'ayer, Tom, and me not kneeling?" asked Twig; and when he received a nod from his brother for answer, the little boy clasped his baby hands together, and said, in a low, timid voice,—

"O dear Dod, do hear us and send a dood angel to take tare of darling Deo. Mother says you will hark to Twiggie, for Desus' sake. Amen."

Silence followed for a few seconds, and then it really seemed as if a good angel must have come to Tom, for he said to Conrad,—

"Here, Connie, just rouse yourself up a bit, and come and catch hold of Twig tightly. Take care of him for your life, and do stop crying. I'm going to get down and run to Farmer Hill's to see if I can't send some one to help Georgie." And almost before he had finished speaking, or they could stop him, Twig was handed over to Conrad, and Tom was on the ground.

He stood still a moment, shook himself together, and then ran—ran as he had never run in his life before. A few minutes sufficed to bring him to Farmer Hill's. There stood the farmer himself, and surely that was Mr. Merton talking to him.

"Father!—Mr. Hill!" shouted the boy, almost breathless now, "Black Prince has broken loose, and

Georgie is on his back down in the lower meadow! Oh, come quickly,—you will be too late!"

The farmer scratched his head in blank amazement. Mr. Merton thought of the false alarm he had received through Tom's means at Mure Hill.

"Why, young master, you be just dreaming now, for Black Prince was safe up in the cow-house with a good strong halter round his neck not half an hour ago."

"Father, O father, indeed 'tis true! Come up here on this mound, and you will see for yourself;" and Tom pulled Mr. Merton up upon a heap of mould, and directed his eyes to the meadow below. Farmer Hill went up too. One glance the two men gave, first at the animal tearing along on its course, regardless of its precious burden, and then at each other. Not a second was wasted. Immediately every available man was called, and down they all hastened to the meadow. Tom was ordered to remain with the farmer's wife, but he, remembering where were his brothers, returned to them, and was standing under the oak tree when the bull dashed at the hedge to get away from its pursuers. The boy felt sick at heart, but roused himself and called to Con to hand Twiggie down, and come down himself, as they had best make haste home. To get Twig safely down was no easy task without Georgie's assistance, especially as the poor little man was so worn out with the fright and his tears that he could do scarcely anything to help himself. Con, too, was not much better; and Tom was, after all, such a small individual, that Twig ran a very good chance of breaking his neck. However, after a large amount of labour on Tom's part, both boys were safely landed on firm ground.

"Now, Con, do for pity's sake shut up that noise; it's no good, you know, and we *must* get home.— That's right, Twiggie; let me wipe your eyes, and we will soon be home. Father must be there by this time, and we shall see how Geo is;" and giving his little brother a kiss, and his big brother a shove onwards, Tom took Twig's hand in his, and the trio started on their way back to Merton House. Poor Tom, he thought he never should get there. Coaxing and scolding both failed at last, and tired out himself, he was on the verge of bursting into tears, when, welcome sound! he heard nurse's voice, and saw figures advancing towards them.

"Oh, my dearies, have not I just been looking for you down by the pond there. I thought you must all be drowned, or torn to pieces by that horrible black bull." And soon Twig was in her strong arms, and nestling his wearied head upon her shoulder.

"Come on, Master Con, there's a good boy! You will soon be home now, and you will catch cold down there. Come on, 'tis only ten minutes to get home." But Conrad, lying crouched up on the damp grass, did not stir, and sobbed out,—

"O nurse! I cannot come home. Oh, I am so wicked! I cannot see father and mother, and—and Geo is killed; and—oh, oh! what shall I do?"

"Miss Georgie is not killed, Master Connie, dear; she is safe in her own bed at home, God be thanked for it, and you cannot stay here all night;—so, John," said she, turning to the coachman, who had come with her to assist in the search, "just take up Master Conrad. I daresay he is tired to death, poor lamb."

Accordingly Con travelled the rest of the way home in the arms of John, whilst Tom trudged on by nurse's side, and detailed to her the events of this memorable afternoon. Mr. Merton met them in the hall, and embraced them fondly, telling them at the same time to go upstairs very softly, so as not to disturb Georgie. They were too worn out and frightened to make any noise, and old nurse begged them off their lessons for that night, gave them tea in the nursery, with as much hot buttered toast as they

could eat, and having taken each to have a peep at
Georgie, who lay quietly sleeping, she marched them
off to bed an hour earlier than usual, not unwillingly
on their part, for their poor wearied eyes could scarcely
keep open. Notwithstanding, however, when Mrs.
Merton went her usual round of their rooms that
night, she was much surprised to find Conrad awake
and crying !

"Why, Connie dear, how is this?   I thought nurse
told me you were asleep hours ago. Do you know
it is nearly one o'clock?   I have been sitting up with
Georgie. She is fast asleep now, and will be pretty
well by to-morrow; so don't cry, my darling boy."

"O mother, I am not crying for Geo, but for myself ! I am such a coward, and so wicked—you don't
know how wicked I am ; and I am so unhappy, and
I cannot go to sleep."

"Now, Con dear, don't worry yourself like this;
and stop crying. Here, let me wash your face; and
drink some of this nice cold water. There now,
dear, I am sure you feel better already. You will be
ill if you cry so much ; it is really silly of you." And
Mrs. Merton tucked up the bed-clothes, smoothed his
pillow, and gave him a fond kiss on his hot forehead.
Soon after, Nature had her way, and he fell into a
deep slumber.

CHAPTER IV.

CON'S CONFESSION.

THE next morning Georgie awoke refreshed by her night's rest, but stiff and sore all over her body, and her ankle pained her greatly. When the doctor came he said she must remain in bed all day, and be carefully looked after.

"Please, Dr. Barton, when shall I be able to walk again? and how long will my ankle go on hurting so much?"

"Indeed I cannot tell you, Miss Georgie; you must submit to being coddled up for a bit. Why it is a wonder every bone in your body was not broken; and a nice job that would have been!"

"But I don't like having to stay here, Dr. Barton."

"Ha! ha! I daresay you don't; but when young ladies take to riding wild bulls, they must submit to being laid up afterwards. Good-bye. Don't use your wrists, mind, more than you can help; and keep up your spirits. Never fear; your ankle will soon

(27)

"I can't help it," muttered her brother.

be well." And the old doctor followed Mrs. Merton out of the room, rubbing his hands together, and smiling to himself.

"I wish you would take a look at Conrad, Dr. Barton. He has a headache, and does not seem at all himself to-day; and last night he did not get to sleep till past one o'clock."

"Sympathy, my dear Mrs. Merton. I expect that is all; and, of course, it must have been a terrible fright for them all."

"Yes, indeed; and the more I think of it, the more wonderful their escape seems. Ah! what might have happened but for our brave Georgie, I cannot bear to even imagine."

"Such a child any mother may well be proud of, Mrs. Merton; but what a pity she was not born the boy instead of the girl."

"I am quite content," said Mrs. Merton, "though I do sometimes wish my Connie were a little more manly. He is such a gentle, delicate little creature; —but here we are;" and opening the nursery door, they entered.

"Here, Con; here is Dr. Barton come to pay you a visit, and cure this dreadful headache. How do you feel now, dear boy?"

"Better, thank you, mother." But he looked very

(27) 4

pale; and the great dark marks under his eyes told of yesterday's weeping.

"Now, young man, just come over to me and let us have a look at you," said the doctor, seating himself in a chair by the window. "Hump! you look as if you had sat up all night. So you have a headache. Ah!" and his cool hand rested a moment on the child's hot forehead. "Now, sir, this is my prescription for you, and I don't think you will say it is a very nasty one. You are to have a holiday to-day and to-morrow, to go out as much as you can; not to be anxious about Georgie, who is nearly all right, or to trouble your mind about anything that is not pleasant. Come, cheer up; I will undertake to have you in capital condition for Miss Acton by the day after to-morrow, if you obey orders. Good-bye, now, and see if you can't smile a bit. You look as if you had all the weight of the world on your young shoulders;" and the kind old doctor gave him a friendly dig in the ribs. But it did no good—smiles seemed for ever banished from the child's sorrowful countenance.

That afternoon during play-time there was quite a little congregation assembled round Georgie's bed. All seemed anxious to do something to make her feel her uncomfortable position less. Alice

brought her a pet story - book; Con, still very
silent and unhappy-looking, placed one of the new
kittens by her side; Tom presented her with a dead
mouse! and little Twig pushed something soft and
sticky into her hand, which proved to be a lump of
barley-sugar. The children were not allowed to
remain long, as Georgie was still very weak, so Miss
Acton soon carried them off to lessons; and nurse
came to sit with her a little time, whilst Mrs. Merton
and Lily went for a short walk. Georgie, feeling
weary, had sunk into a kind of half slumber, when
foot-steps entering her room disturbed her, and, raising her heavy eyelids, she beheld her father bending
over the bed.

"Well, Georgie, how do you feel now? Were you
asleep? I am so sorry if I awoke you!"

"No, father; I was not exactly asleep. I feel
rather tired and achy all over me; but I daresay
I shall be all right to-morrow."

"I trust you will, my child. I am sure I feel
truly thankful you are alive. But what have you got
there struggling about in that frantic style?"

"Oh, it is only the kitten, father. Con brought it
to me. He thought it would amuse me; but I did not
feel well enough to play with it. Will you give it
to nurse, and she will take it downstairs to its

mother? I thought I heard Topsy mew just now, so perhaps she is in a fright about it."

"Nurse is gone to have her tea; but I am going down as soon as she comes back, and I will relieve poor Topsy's fears myself. Georgie, do you know if anything has gone wrong with Con? He tells you all his secrets, I know; is there anything worrying him at present except your being laid up? He is in such bad spirits, and we can't get a word out of him."

"I do not know of anything, father; he was all right yesterday. He must be bothering himself about me. I wish he wouldn't, for I can't bear for him to be unhappy."

"Well, dear, will you like to talk to him a bit, if you feel equal to it, and see what is the matter? He is doing no lessons to-day.—Here is nurse, with some tea and very nice-looking sponge-cake, which I daresay you will like very much."

"Please sir, it is cocoa, not tea. I thought Miss Georgie would like it best, so I made her some."

"Quite right, nurse; invalids should always have what they like best. See her take it, and then you may send Master Conrad to sit here a bit.—Now, Georgie, I want that kitten. But what's this? Uch! a dead mouse! How in the world did that come here?"

"Oh, please, father, don't say anything; it was Tom brought it to comfort me, and I did not like to say no, though it does not smell very nice. I think Carlo killed it three days ago; we tried to find it in the hay-loft, but could not, and Tom said he discovered it this morning, and thought I should like it."

"A dead mouse to comfort you!" repeated Mr. Merton. "Well, of all the strange modes of comfort I ever heard of, that is the strangest. I really must stop Tom adopting such methods in future."

"O father, please don't say anything to Tom; he did not know he was doing wrong, and really I did not mind."

"Very well then, Georgie; but now try to take your cocoa and sponge-cake; and good-bye for the present."

Mr. Merton bent down, kissed Georgie, took up the kitten in one hand and the mouse by its tail in the other, and left the room.

Half an hour later, Con was sitting on Georgie's bed, nursing his knees, and his chin resting on them. It was twilight now, and though the day was warm without, a bright fire burned in the room, and cast strange shadows over the walls. There had been a long silence. Con seemed disinclined to enter upon a conversation; whilst Georgie, refreshed by her cocoa, felt better, and desirous to talk.

"What's the matter, Con? You look as grave as a judge. If it were not for my ankle, I would kick you. Cheer up, old man; I shall be right enough in a few days, so don't go plaguing yourself about me."

" I'm not," was all the answer she received; and silence again reigned.

"Con," said Georgie at last, "can't you talk to me? It is awfully dull lying here, you know. I wish you wouldn't be so glum. Does your head ache? or what in the world is the matter with you?"

" I can't help it," muttered her brother in a low voice.

Several minutes now elapsed before Georgie made another effort. She watched the shadows on the opposite wall. Next she counted the ornaments on the chimney-piece. After that she tried to reckon the books on the shelf; but failing to distinguish them easily, she spoke again; this time in rather a hurt voice, and with a half sob as she commenced,—

" I think you are very unkind, Con; you would not like to feel as ill as I do; and I should not treat you like this."

Then at last the boy seemed to recover himself; and stooping down, he kissed his sister several times, and said eagerly,—

"Oh, Georgie, I don't know what has come over me! I cannot make out. I seem to do everything wrong. I am a coward, I tell lies, I am unkind to you! Georgie, Georgie, tell me what *am* I to do?"

"You are a coward! you tell lies!" repeated Georgie in a tone of utter amazement. "What *do* you mean? Tell me directly."

"It is quite true, Geo, quite true; and I will tell you all about it. I must tell some one, and I had better tell you." So saying, he moved slowly off the bed, walked to the door, looked out, shut it again, and then seated himself once more on the bed.

"What did you do that for?" inquired Georgie.

"I wanted to see that no one was outside in the passage, who could anyhow overhear what I am going to tell you."

"Who was likely to be there, I should like to know? But go on, make haste. I want to hear what this is all about."

"Well, Georgie, don't be in a hurry, and I will begin at the beginning. You remember, the day before yesterday, Lily left her knitting in the drawing-room, and sent me down to get it. She wanted to show Miss Acton something about the heel of Tom's sock—you recollect, don't you? Well, I went down all right, found the knitting, and was just leaving

the room, when I thought I saw something moving
on the chiffonier. I went across to see what it was,
and discovered a curious little glass-box with a live
big beetle-looking thing in it, kicking about its legs
like anything. I was awfully surprised, and could
not make it out a bit. Have you seen it, Georgie?"

"No, no; of course not. Go on," answered she
impatiently.

"Just when I was looking at this strange thing, I
heard Lily calling out to me to make haste; so I put
it down very carefully just where I found it, and
went up with the knitting. Yesterday morning, you
know, we had half an hour's play after breakfast,
when we had a run in the garden. Do you remember I said to you, after we had been out a few
minutes, that I should run back to get my knife?"

"Yes," said Georgie, breathlessly, "I remember you
wanted it to cut those sticks for the dove's perches."

"Yes, so I said," proceeded Con; "but, Georgie,
that was all a make-up. I did not really want it. The
truth is, that beetle thing had been in my head all
the morning, and try as I would, I could not get it
out; so I determined to run back to the drawing-
room, to see if it were still there. I knew mother
and Lily would not be there then, so I could see for
myself. I got safely enough into the house and into

the drawing-room. The glass-box was just where I had left it the day before. I examined it again, and still could not make out how it could live and move in a box with no air in it. The legs did go at such a rate, Georgie, you can't think! and there was no pin or anything I could see to make it stay; only some bits of grass and flower stuff. Suddenly I heard a row; and there was Carlo rolling himself on the white rug; and he was so dirty, you know, yesterday! I felt awfully frightened, for father says Carlo is not to come in-doors at all, and not into the drawing-room above all places. As quick as possible I put down the beetle, and was just going to rush to turn Carlo out, when—when—oh, Georgie, I cannot tell you!"

"Go on!" said his sister authoritatively.

"O Georgie, only think! my horrid sleeve caught in that vase of father's! I dragged it down, and— and I broke that great piece out!"

"O Con, Connie!" cried poor Georgie; "and you said you did NOT do it!"

Until this moment, she had never given another thought to the broken vase, since her mother had questioned her about it; consequently the shock was very great. She sat up in bed and gazed at her brother with a piteous expression. He could not bear to meet her honest blue eyes, now full of reproach, even in this dimly-lighted room; so he buried his face in the bed-clothes, and uttered not a word.

"Con," said Georgie, after the lapse of a few minutes, "you must go straight and tell father; do you hear?"

Slowly and deliberately Con raised himself, clasped his hands tightly together, and answered, "I dare not!" He then once more hid his face in the comforting bed-clothes.

"But you must; indeed you must. Oh, Con, do think what an awful story you told mother, and *twice* over. Whatever made you do it? Why did not you say it was an accident? Con, you must go and confess about it to father; it is the only thing you can do now."

"I cannot go," replied a smothered voice; "I feel ashamed. I am afraid of what father will say. I said 'no' twice over, so that it was two stories. Oh, how could I have been so wicked? The first 'no' came out whilst I was thinking if I could venture to tell; and then, when mother asked us the second time, I felt that then I must say 'no' too, as I had said it before."

"You were dreadfully wicked, Con; and you must try to make up for it by telling the truth now.

All the truth, I mean—everything about it. It is the only thing you can do;—don't you see it yourself, darling?" and Georgie passed her hand over her brother's head in a caressing manner. The boy's frame shook; he longed to cry, but was determined, if possible, to keep back his tears, and with a desperate effort he succeeded.

"I would come with you, Connie dear, if it were not for my ankle; but I don't think I can manage to stand on it."

Con raised himself now, and getting up from the bed, said in rather a trembling voice, "Of course you are not to think of such a thing, Georgie. I must go alone; I see I must." He walked as far as the door, then stopped.

"Go on, Con; be a brave boy!" called out Georgie. But it was no good; his spirit failed him, and returning to the bed-side, he flung himself on his knees, and burst into an agony of tears. His sister lay back on her pillow; she was well-nigh exhausted, but her will was strong, and her sense of right stronger still.

"It must be done," thought she to herself. "My poor Con! I cannot bear to see him in such trouble, and be obliged to stay here and do nothing to help him. I wonder, if I could get downstairs with him

if it would hurt my ankle very much. If I had
something warm over my shoulders I couldn't catch
cold. Yes, I think I'll try.—Con, look here; get up a
minute,"—she had already thrown the clothes off, and
was sitting on the opposite side of the bed to where
her brother was crouching, with her legs dangling
out. " Just find something warm to go over me, and
one of my slippers. I have made up my mind; I
am going down with you."

Con sprang up at these words, and stared at his
sister in utter astonishment. He had been so much
engaged with his own tears that he had not noticed
her movements.

"But, Georgie, you must not; indeed you must
not," he gasped out.

"Hold your tongue, sir, and just do as you are
told! I do as I choose. There are my slippers over
there. I only want one, as I shan't want anything
over my bad foot, for I shan't walk on it. Now,
then, what can I have to keep me warm? What is
there?"

"I don't know," said Con slowly. " Yes, I do
though. Wait a minute, Georgie,"—and he rushed
out of the room, soon returning with a great bundle
in his arms.

" Why, Con, that's Norman's ulster."

"Yes, I know; but I thought it would be just the very thing to keep you jolly warm. I expect it is too long, but we can tuck it up."

Accordingly Georgie was arrayed in this strange costume. It was, indeed, much too long, for Norman was six feet high; but the extra length was fastened up round the waist by the band, which was tied in a big knot to prevent its slipping. Georgie was at last ready, and by dint of hopping and holding on to Con, she reached the door and the top of the staircase in safety. Arrived there, Georgie said she did not think she could hop down; the lights and the movement made her feel funny; so she proposed that they should both sit down on the staircase and slip down one step at a time. In this way they reached the hall without interruption.

"I say, Georgie, they must be still in at dinner," whispered Con. "Do you think we had better go in?"

"Of course," said his sister in a most decided manner. "I have not come down here for nothing, I can tell you. Come on;—oh! my ankle has begun to hurt so. Make haste; there's a dear."

The dining-room door was reached—how, they did not know—and the pair entered. A general exclamation greeted them, and no wonder. Georgie in her

comical attire, her hair all rough as she had risen
from her bed, no stockings on, only one shoe, her
white night-dress showing, her blue eyes gleaming
with excitement, deep black marks underneath them,
her face ghastly pale, save one burning spot on each
cheek, standing on one leg, leant on her brother,
whose tear-stained and frightened-looking little face
seemed to betoken some great trouble.

"My dearest children, what is the matter?—Georgie,
how could you get out of bed? How did you come
down? Here, let me help you on to this sofa at
once."

"No, no, father and mother, I am all right, and
came down all right.—Be quiet, Lily!—I can stand
without your assistance, thank you, Norman.—Now,
Con, speak out like a man."

"Please, father," said the boy, in a voice scarcely
raised above a whisper—"please, father"—and then
he stopped.

"Make haste, Con; do be quick. Oh!"—and poor
Georgie with much difficulty repressed an audible
groan, her ankle was hurting her so badly.

"Please, father, it was I broke your vase—I am
very, very sorry," at length brought out Con in one
breath, for Georgie was pulling his arm so very hard.
His confession made, he dared not raise his eyes, but

turned them to his sister, who said in a faint voice, "That's my own Con!" and then fell back insensible into the arms of Norman, who had never ceased watching her, and, appreciating the tremendous restraint the child was putting upon herself, was more prepared than the rest of the party for this result. A heart-rending cry burst from Con.

"She's dead! she's dead! Oh, why did I not make her stay in bed! Why did I let her come down!"

"Conrad," said Mr. Merton, "cease that noise, and go and remain in the library till I come to you. Georgie is not dead; she has only fainted."

He added the last part of his speech out of compassion to the wild look of terror in the boy's eyes. Meanwhile Norman had carried Georgie up to her own room, placed her tenderly in bed, and then resigning her to the care of his mother, Lily, and nurse, he went downstairs to rejoin his father. Half an hour later Lily came down and reported that Georgie had recovered consciousness, but seemed very excited. Before night she was so feverish that the doctor was sent for, and pronounced her to be in a state of nervous fever, brought on by the excitement and exertion to which she had been subjected.

Meanwhile we must not forget the poor little culprit who was the unwilling cause of all this anxiety.

Mr. Merton left him to his own reflections for about an hour, and then went to see after him. Con was crumpled up in a chair, looking the picture of misery. When his father entered he did not move, but remained in precisely the same position.

"Conrad," at last said Mr. Merton, who had placed himself in his favourite arm-chair, and had spent a few minutes in watching the child—"Conrad, come here. What have you got to say for yourself?"

The boy got down, and slowly advanced towards him.

"Do you know, my boy, you have been exceedingly naughty?"

"Yes, father."

"What made you act so, Conrad? You know far better, for you are not a little baby, but a big boy twelve years old."

"Please, father, I was afraid."

"O Conrad, how many, many times have your mother and I told you, if you met with an accident of that kind, always to come at once and tell us of it. Then, however much we may be distressed about it, we will pass the matter over. My boy, you are a coward, and cowardice is a thing every boy and man should be ashamed of. How will you ever get through your life, if you are afraid of even your own parents? Why is it you act so foolishly?"

"Father, indeed I do try to be braver, and Georgie is always telling me about it; but it seems to be no good, for I always feel just as frightened when the next time comes,—and, indeed, indeed, I did not mean to tell the story."

"That is no excuse, my son, none whatever. Now, listen to me, and you will see you really must strive against this failing of yours more than you have ever done hitherto. First, you disobeyed by not telling your parents of your misfortune; and then you told two wilful falsehoods, which caused you to sin deeply, not only against your earthly parents, but against your Father in heaven. Next, you did not confess your sin of your own accord; you were afraid to do so. You, a boy, required your poor sick sister to assist you in doing so! You told the truth then, it is true, but Georgie will feel the effects of her endeavours in your behalf for some time. She is very ill now, and the doctor has been sent for. Don't cry; it will do no good. This illness of Georgie's is the punishment that God has sent you. I shall add no other, but this I shall require of you, that, to-morrow morning, after prayers, before the servants have left the room (for, remember, suspicion fell on them), you declare, in a clear, distinct voice, so that all may hear you, that you alone were the person who broke my

(27) 5

vase although you did deny it; and express your sorrow for so doing."

"O father, father!" sobbed the unhappy Con, "that is harder than any punishment. What shall I do— what shall I do?"

"I will tell you what you shall do, my dear child. You shall kneel down here and say your evening prayers, and we will both ask that strength may be given you, not only to do what I expect of you to-morrow, but to make you a brave boy in future."

Kneeling together side by side, the father and the son prayed; and when they rose, both felt comforted.

"Good-night now, my poor boy. Go quickly to sleep, and rise in the morning with a determination to be a 'victor in the strife.'" So saying, Mr. Merton pressed a loving kiss on Con's forehead, and dismissed him, for the hour of his ordinary bed-time had long since passed.

CHAPTER V.

E will not follow Georgie through the long and tedious illness which was the result of all her exploits. She was never in a dangerous state, but was yet so ill that she required constant watching night and day. It was fortunate for her that she had so many kind nurses at hand. Miss Acton took her part, and really seemed far more at home as a sick nurse than in her ordinary vocation. She was gentle, quiet, patient, and never apparently fatigued. The spirits which to the children she always appeared to lack in every-day life, would have been out of place in the sick-room: at the same time, when necessary, she was always bright and cheerful, so that Georgie was ever glad when she entered.

One day, when the invalid was growing into convalescence, and had been partially dressed and placed on a sofa near the window. Miss Acton came in to relieve Mrs. Merton, who had been with her some hours. Georgie was very thin and pale, and altogether a good deal changed from when we first introduced her to our readers. Miss Acton held in her hand a very pretty little moss basket filled with sweet-scented flowers; for the time had flown by quickly, and the month of May was nearly gone.

"What lovely flowers, Miss Acton! and what a dear little basket! Did you make it yourself?"

"Yes, dear. It is long since I made one, and I had almost forgotten the way, but I thought you would like it, and coming upon some pretty moss in our early morning walk, put the idea into my mind."

"Oh, thank you so much; it is beautifully made."

"Would you like me to go on reading to you, Georgie? You were interested in the story yesterday; or would you rather that I only talked?"

"No, please go on reading, Miss Acton, if you won't find it a bother."

The governess fetched the book, and, seating herself in a chair at Georgie's feet, commenced. She read well; the tale was a stirring one, and she seemed to enter into it fully. Georgie looked at her in wonder, as she watched her eyes sparkle, and the colour rise to the usually pallid cheeks, whilst ever and anon a bright smile pervaded her whole face, putting into it such an expression as the child had never marked there before. At last the daylight began to wane, the book was closed, and the reader seemed for the time lost in thought. Georgie gave a little sigh. Miss Acton roused herself, and in a moment remembered where she was. She arose from her seat, gently smoothed the invalid's pillows, provided her with some slight refreshment, and gave her a long, lingering kiss.

"Miss Acton," said Georgie, in turn rousing herself, "what makes you so kind to me? I am sure when I was well I was always bothering you. I don't deserve a bit for you to be so nice to me."

For answer she received only another kiss, and a tender squeeze of the hand.

"I want to know why you are so jolly now, dear Miss Acton," persisted Georgie. "You were not always so," she added somewhat bluntly. "I did not use to care about you, but now everything seems different."

"It is seeing you lying there so helpless, dear Georgie. It brings back to me the days of my own childhood, when my sister Rose was laid up with a sprained ankle, and I used to pretend to be her nurse."

"What kind of things did you do when you were

a little girl? I suppose you did not get into scrapes like as I do."

"Well, no, I cannot say I used to get into the sort of troubles you do, Georgie; but still I am afraid very often I was a very tiresome child."

"Do tell me about some of your adventures, Miss Acton. I feel so tired, and it would amuse me so much, if you don't mind."

"Not a bit, if you care to hear them, dear Georgie. You know we were not a large family, only three of us—my brother, who is now a clergyman, my sister Rose, and myself. I was the middle one, for Rose was older and Horace younger than I was. We were brought up very strictly, but never seemed to mind it, for we loved our father dearly. Our mother died when our youngest little sister was born, so our Aunt Jane came to live with us, to help father to bring us up. She was an old maid, many years older than mother, and I am afraid we used to plague her dreadfully, though we could not help loving her at the same time. I remember one day when my brother got into trouble particularly well. Aunt Jane used to wear very high lace caps, and lots of stiff little curls down each side of her face. We children made up our minds that these said curls must be false; they were so beautifully tidy always, and so black.

At last, one night just as Rose and I had gone into bed, Horace suddenly appeared at the door in his night-gown, and said,—

"'Girls, are you asleep?'

"'No,' we answered softly.

"'Well, just listen to me, then; a capital idea has come into my mind about finding out if the Aged's curls are real.' Horace was only eight, so of course it was very disrespectful of him to speak of Aunt Jane in this manner; but he always would do so, and no one, not even father, could break him of the trick.

"Of course, we were very much interested in what he said, so we asked him to come closer to our bed, that we might hear better what he was saying.

"'Now listen,' said he, 'this is my plan: I am going to be late to-morrow morning for prayers; it will get me into a row, I know, but that can't be helped. Mind, you girls are to wonder why I am not down,—such a good boy as I am,—something must be the matter, and all that sort of thing, you know! Well, the Aged always goes out of the library first, straight across the hall to the dining-room, whilst the servants are standing there. It will be splendid! I am going to stand on the staircase with my fishing-rod in my hand;—but hark! surely that's father's step! Be fast asleep, girls. I put my pillow to sleep in my bed, and he is sure not to have a candle.' And then that naughty Horace crept under our bed; and when father came into the room, we two girls, who were just as bad as he was, pretended to be asleep.

"We heard father come in and mutter to himself, 'The children are quiet enough. Jane must have been mistaken, as usual.'

"He then went to Horace's room, and seemed quite satisfied there also, for a few seconds later we heard him going downstairs again. As soon as the footsteps died away, Horace's voice said in a whisper from under the bed, 'Good-night, girls; I daren't stay. Do you think I can venture out now?'

"'Yes,' we answered; and a rush of a little white figure told us of his escape, and the next instant we could distinguish a kind of low, hushed whistle, that was meant to telegraph to us the news that he was once more safely in bed.

"To-morrow morning came, and we went down in good time, but Horace was not visible. Aunt Jane and father asked whether we knew the reason of his non-appearance. For answer we obeyed the directions we had received the night before. We felt, as you may imagine, greatly excited during prayers,

though we were bound to be quiet. Our hearts beat
so quickly when they were ended, and Aunt Jane
advanced to the door held open for her as usual by
one of the servants. We followed; and father came
last. We were in the hall when—O Georgie, I never
shall forget it, if I live to be a hundred!—we suddenly beheld, almost before we were prepared for it,
the line of the fishing-rod come down over the
banisters, and rest for a second on Aunt Jane's cap.
It then gave a little jerk, and in another moment we
beheld the cap floating in mid air, and our poor aunt
standing speechless and motionless with horror; the
back of her head only covered with a few whitish
hairs, and the lovely curls and black hair in front
remaining unruffled as usual. Our object was
achieved; there could be no doubt now but that it
was false. We felt dreadfully frightened, all the
same, as to what the consequences of this mad performance might be; and I am afraid they would
have been rather serious for Horace, had not father
who had a keen sense of the ridiculous, burst into
fits of laughter, which he could not repress. We all
laughed then, we could not help it; and Aunt Jane,
dear good-natured old soul, thought the best thing
she could do was to laugh too. Meanwhile the
unfortunate cap was being jerked up and down in a

most extraordinary style, and I don't think there would have been much of it left whole, had not I rushed upstairs and told Horace that the only thing he could do now was to come down at once, ask Aunt Jane's pardon, and present her with the precious cap whilst it was yet uninjured. This he accordingly did, fishing-rod in hand, requesting at the same time to be allowed the supreme pleasure of replacing the cap in its proper place on Aunt Jane's head. He was permitted to do so; and though father gave him a long lecture that evening about performing such tricks, he escaped punishment,— which was far more than he deserved. What think you, Georgie?"

"Well, he certainly was rather a naughty boy," she replied; and judging from her animated, happy face, she must have enjoyed the little story immensely. "But go on, please, Miss Acton, do tell us something else you did; you and your brother and sister, I mean."

"Let me see; what shall I tell you? Oh, I know Once we had another little sister, called Violet; she was such a darling, we never could make enough of her. Horace was extremely jealous of her at first: he was two and a half when she was born, and did not at all approve of being the baby no longer.

"'Nasty 'ittle t'ing,' he used to call her. 'Take her 'way; me is a nice dood boy; that only uggy 'ittle dirl.'

"One day the nurse found him busily engaged in covering the poor baby over, as she lay asleep in her little cradle, with shawls, cushions, muffs, toys,—in fact, everything he could lay his hands on. Nurse had turned her back for a few minutes, so had not perceived what he had been doing.

"'Oh, Master Horace,' she cried out, 'you must not do that; you will kill the baby.'

"'Me no tare,' answered the jealous boy; 'me no tare if me till baby! Den ev'y one lub Horrie; no one lub him now.'"

"What a wicked boy!" interrupted Georgie. "I would have given him a good slap, if I had been the nurse. Fancy, wanting to kill his little sister!"

"But then you see, dear, Horace was only a baby himself, and did not know right from wrong. However, he was not always so jealous of her; for when she grew older, and began to notice, no one in the whole house made more fuss about ''ittle tarling Vi' than did Horace.

"But I was going to tell you about an adventure she had, when she was about three and a half years old. She was going with father and Aunt Jane to

stay with some cousins who lived near London. It
was a long journey for such a dot to take, but father
wanted to take her so much that it was determined
she should go. She slept all the first part of the
journey, and when she awoke she felt in such good
spirits that there was no keeping her quiet. However, the other passengers did not seem to mind her
frolicsome goings on, except one gouty old gentleman,
who said to himself, for no one noticed him, that he
wished railway companies had separate carriages for
children, they were always in the way. At last she
became quieter, and sat for a long time on father's
lap, busily engaged in playing with his beard, twist-
ing and plaiting it in the most extraordinary manner.
When she grew weary of this amusement, she
slipped down off father's knee, and stood on tiptoe
looking out of the window. Suddenly the train gave
a jerk, the door flew open, and before father or any
one could do aught to save her, Violet had fallen out!
It was the work of an instant. Father was like one
gone mad, and would have jumped out after her, had
not the other passengers held him back. Aunt Jane
shut the door close, and sought for the signal cord,
but alas! none was to be found. The train was
going on and on. The gouty gentleman exerted
himself to his utmost, and yelled out of his window

as long as he could.   Father and Aunt Jane screamed
out of the other.   At last some of the other passengers
in the other carriages heard them, and they, thinking
the train was on fire, shouted out also.   The train
had gone a mile and a half before the guard heard
them, and then it was stopped to know what was
the matter.   This was quickly explained, and father,
Aunt Jane, and two or three of the passengers were
put down, and hastened as quickly as they could
back to the spot where Violet had fallen out.   Father
arrived first, but no sign of her was to be seen.

"'We have missed the place,' he cried.   'My
darling child!   What shall we do?'

"Aunt Jane maintained, however, that this was the
exact spot where the accident had happened; and
whilst she was speaking, a labourer appeared, who,
politely touching his cap, asked if he could be of any
use.

"Father immediately said, 'Oh, my man, have you
seen my little child?   She fell out of the train just
gone by, and now we cannot find—even her body,'
and then poor father groaned and covered his eyes
with his hands.

"'If you please, your honour, maybe you can tell
me if she be a little lady with a lot of yella hair, and
a bluish frock like?'

" ' Yes, yes,' cried every one ; ' where is she ?'

" ' I do know where she was then, half an hour agone; for I seed her with Bill Robinson, and I thought to myself, I wonder now where he picked up with that smart little crittur. I can show you where his cottage be, if your honour pleases.'

"The party then made their way over some ploughed fields, and soon came in sight of two very small cottages standing together, far away apparently from any other habitation. 'That be my cottage, and that Bill Robinson's,' they were duly informed by their guide. They reached the gate leading up through the patch of garden to Robinson's house. Father's hand was shaking so he could not undo the latch, when the front door opened, and Violet herself, unharmed and looking perfectly well, appeared ! She ran to meet us, and did not seem in the least disturbed. Father snatched her up in his arms and covered her with kisses ; whilst Aunt Jane's eyes filled with tears of thankfulness.

" Mrs. Robinson soon put in an appearance, a tidy, clean sort of woman, and gave an account of how Violet had come into her hands. 'My Bill,' she said, 'brought her in. He told me as how he had seen her fall out of the train, from a field hard by, and had gone to see after her. When he comed up, the little lady was sitting on the bank, not crying, sir, but trying to wipe the dust off her pretty frock! He asked if she was hurt, and who she might be; and so she told him, quite possessed like, that she was Miss Violet Hacton, and was going to visit her cousins in Lunnon, only she would like to go somewhere first to have her frock cleaned. So then my goodman guessed as how 'twould be best to bring her on here, and he asked her if she would please to come, and offered to carry her. She told him his hands were dirty, so she would walk; but her bits of legs soon grew tired going over the rough ground, and she was glad enough to be carried. When she got here I cleaned her frock, and washed her bonny face and hands; and then, as she said she was thirsty, I gived her a drop of milk to drink. 'Twas all I could do, sir, for I guessed some one would come to see after her.'

"This was all the explanation she gave. Father gave her a handsome present, and was just taking his leave, with wee Violet still in his arms, when honest Bill himself came up, and said he was right thankful to see them there, for he had been along the line to look out for any one coming back, but thought, as he had met no one, the little lady might have to spend the night in their cottage, 'which ain't fit for the likes of she,' he added.

"Father thanked him much for his kindness, and having also given a present to the labourer who had acted as guide, he and the rest of the party hastened back to the line by a short cut that Robinson pointed out to them, and there found waiting a carriage and small engine in readiness to convey them to the next station, some five miles distant."

"What a wonderful escape, Miss Acton. What could have saved her? I thought people were always killed who fell out of trains when they were going on."

"Yes, dear, it did indeed seem marvellous, and it could only have been little Violet's light weight that saved her, for she alighted quite safely on some grass some three or four yards from the embankment."

"Was not she hurt a bit?"

"No; when they got to London, a doctor was sent for, but he declared she had suffered no injury whatever, except a slight scratch on one of her wrists."

"How happy you must all have been. But she did not live much longer, did she?"

"No, she died when she was nearly five; three-quarters past four, as she used to call herself. About a week before her death she was out with Horace in the garden flying a kite. 'Horrie,' she said, 'very soon I am going up into the blue sky, much higher

than your kite, right up into heaven.' Dear little
pet, we did not think then that her words would
really come true. Scarlet fever came into our village.
Father, you know, was the vicar. We all took it,
but had it very mildly, except Violet, who was only
taken ill one Saturday, and the Monday evening she
died. Poor father, we thought he never would get
over the shock. His hair turned so white, and for a
long, long time, he never smiled. When his last
hour came, he said to us three, who were standing
round his bed, 'Children, I shall see your mother
and my little blossom. I feel so happy.'—Ah, dear
father, how we miss you, more than your little
one!"

Tears stole down Miss Acton's face, not many, but
Georgie discovered them even in the darkness.

"Come here," she said; and obediently the governess
came and knelt down by her side. "Miss Acton,
when I get well again, I am going to try not to tease
you any more; and if you will let me, I think I shall
love you very much, you have been so jolly and kind
to me ever since I have been ill."

"Indeed, dear Georgie, 'tis but little I have ever
done for you," faltered Miss Acton.

There was silence for a short time, and then
Georgie said rather deliberately,—

"Miss Acton, will you be offended if I tell you something?"

"No, dear; what is it?"

"Just this, that if you, when you see me getting into one of my mad fits, would just talk a little—mind, you promised not to be offended—a little *faster*, I am certain, quite certain, I should not care to plague you half so much. I know I am very naughty sometimes; but then you are always the same in your manner, whether I am good or whether I am naughty, so awfully quiet, that I do long, just for the excitement, to try to aggravate you. I'll not try to do so any more though."

Miss Acton could not repress a smile. Sorrow in her young life seemed to have banished all spirits out of her, and she had acquired a slow, measured way of speaking; of which failing she was well aware. She had thought, poor woman, that it suited her to speak thus in her capacity as governess, and little dreamed how much it annoyed her pupils. She could not feel hurt at Georgie's funny way of telling her of it, so she told the child that in future she would talk to her, when she saw her inclined to be naughty, "like a steam-engine."

Georgie laughed merrily at this, and promised in return to become good "in a minute."

Miss Acton had not much faith in her promises, but nevertheless they sounded very pleasant, and when presently nurse came to put the invalid to bed, she felt quite sorry so happy an evening had come to an end.

CHAPTER VI.

ILL TEMPER.

THE Mertons were a happy, loving family, on the whole, warmly devoted to one another. The sound of quarrelling was an extraordinary and forbidden thing amongst them; but it sometimes happens even in the best regulated families that a storm does arise, though it may be quickly followed by a calm more tranquil than existed before.

One day, in the summer holidays, it was arranged that a long-promised excursion should take place to an old castle some little distance off. The rector and his family were asked to join the party, and a very pleasant day was anticipated. There seemed no chance of rain, and the night before every one retired to bed early. Georgie and Tom adopted the peculiar plan of fastening their big toes by means of a string to the ends of their beds, in order that they might awaken in good time! Conrad tried it also, but found it so uncomfortable,—for every time he moved in bed, he felt as if his toe would be pulled off,—that he undid the string, and having set his poor toe at liberty, he soon fell asleep.

The day broke, the sun shone forth, and the weather promised to be most beautiful. Breakfast was not till eight, but the young folks were up and dressed soon after six o'clock, and making so much row in the house that at last nurse turned them out of doors into the garden, where they might make as much noise as they liked without disturbing any one. There were two ways of reaching Luttone Castle,—by the river, or by the more direct road through the village and over Luttone Bridge. It was arranged that the provisions should be conveyed by the shorter road in the donkey-cart, and that the party themselves should go by water. Accordingly, at half-past nine o'clock, quite a large number were assembled on the rectory lawn, which sloped down to the banks of the river, and possessed also a very convenient landing-place.

There were present Mr. and Mrs. Merton; the rector and Mrs. Armstrong; Lily, Alice, Georgie, Conrad, and Tom Merton (Twig was not allowed to come, as it was thought such a long day would only tire him. so he was left behind with nurse); Margaret

Armstrong, Lily's great friend, a girl about her own age; Jack and Victor Armstrong, two public school boys about fifteen and sixteen; and their youngest sister Elsie, a quiet, gentle girl, who admired Georgie from a distance, and was invariably to be found by Alice's side. Off they started at last, and a very merry party they were. There were two boats ready to convey them. Mr. Merton and Jack Armstrong rowed one, with Lily to steer; and the rector and his younger son rowed the other, with Tom acting as steersman. Certainly Tom's steering was peculiar; he was for ever pulling one or the other string too much, and no less than three times did he drive his boat straight into the bank! However, no harm happened, and in about an hour they passed safely under the arches of Luttone Bridge, and drew up at the landing-place. From hence to the castle was a good steep ascent; the river formed part of the ancient moat, and a splendid fortress it must have been in the olden days. It was past eleven o'clock before they reached the top, and found themselves under the shade of the massive walls. They were all fairly tired, for the sun was pouring down, and the climb up over the heated, slippery turf had been no light task, so they sat down for some little time to rest themselves. Presently the young ones began to grow restless, and to wander about within the castle. They were told that about one o'clock they would hear a whistle, when they were all to return at once for dinner, and meanwhile the parents of both families would sit quietly where they were, enjoying the cool, and indulging in a cosy chat. It was a long time, some years, in fact, since they had been here, and to Tom everything was new, for on the last occasion he had been considered too young to come. Now he was wild with excitement. Lily and Margaret wandered together arm in arm. Alice was bent on making some discovery either of coins or other relics.

"You may laugh if you like, Jack, but I feel perfectly certain that lots of treasures are to be found in this place. I have heard father say so many times."

"Doubtless," answered Jack, with a low bow; "and will it please your ladyship to point out the kind of spots, now, where your superior knowledge would induce you to suppose such treasures might be concealed. I can assure you I would dig with the greatest pleasure for you, if I thought I could aid you in making any such important discovery."

"Well, now," answered Alice with great confidence, "that mound over yonder cannot have come of itself.

It must have been made for some object, and who
can doubt that it was for the purpose of covering up
something beneath it."

The Armstrong boys looked at each other, and
burst into fits of laughter.   Alice felt rather hurt at
their behaviour, so she turned away into another part
of the castle, and left the boys and Georgie to their
own devices, contenting herself with the fact that
at any rate Elsie believed in what she said. The two
friends entered the keep, and, ascending an old
rickety staircase, they at last reached the top of the
highest of the towers, from whence they had a
splendid view of the surrounding country. There
were slight railings placed round to prevent accidents,
so there they seated themselves, and soon being
engaged in a close conversation, became utterly
oblivious to the actions of the rest of the party.
At last it struck them that the dinner-hour must
be approaching, so very carefully they descended
the stairs, but, lo! behold! when they reached the
bottom, they found the door bolted from the outside.
Here was a pleasant predicament for them to be in;
prisoners in truth they were, and with no chance of
escape.

" I wonder who can have done this," said Alice. " I
never heard any one come into the keep."

"Neither did I," said Elsie; "but of course it is only one of the boys who has done it for a joke. They are sure to let us out again, when the whistle sounds for dinner."

"I am not so sure it is one of the boys," replied Alice in a mysterious voice. "You know, Elsie, very often bad men come into old places like this, and do all sorts of wicked things. There was a child murdered here once; I heard nurse say so."

"Don't talk like that," said Elsie, really frightened now. "Had not we better go up to the top again and shout?"

"Well, it would be the best thing, I suppose. At any rate it would show we were not without friends here."

Accordingly upstairs they once more journeyed, and called out to Mr. Merton and Mr. Armstrong by name, believing that by so doing the robbers or whoever the wretches were would be overawed, and afraid to come and do them any harm. They then came down again, prepared to shake and kick at the door with all their strength, when, curious to relate, there it stood wide open, and not a person in sight!

"This is most extraordinary," said Alice, looking everywhere about; "it proves that I am right, and that it could not have been the boys, for we must have both seen and heard them. I suppose it was not a ghost, for I don't believe in them, and besides they only walk about at night."

"I am sure I don't know," replied Elsie; "but hark! surely that's the dinner-bell—whistle, I mean. We had better make haste."

"Yes, come on; but mind and don't say anything about our being locked in till I give you leave."

"All right," answered Elsie; and in a few minutes they had reached the shady spot, where a most delightful-looking repast had been spread out, and where every other member of the family had already assembled. Seeing this, the two girls exchanged glances, but said nothing. They were greeted with exclamations on their lateness, and inquiries as to where they had been.

"Only on the top of the high tower," replied Alice, without looking up, or she could not have helped noticing a little by-play that was going on amongst the younger ones at the other end of the table-cloth,—for, of course, there was no table. Soon all were engaged in feasting on the good things provided, and all felt the better for their refreshment; whilst, as is usual on such occasions, no end of little pleasantries arose, which provoked much merriment.

After the meal was ended, it was proposed that the whole party should start on an exploring expedi-

tion; and Jack amused every one very much by
walking in advance with a great pickaxe over his
shoulder, which he declared he had borrowed from
the old man who had charge of the castle, in order
to be ready to find the treasures which Alice had
told him were concealed there. In and out of the
different rooms they wandered, all round the keep,
and were just crossing the court-yard when they came
upon the mound they had noticed that morning.
Jack immediately went up to Mr. Merton, and asked
him if he seriously thought that it would be worth
while to dig into it a little, just to see if there were
any vestige of ancient remains to be found.

"I am afraid there is not the remotest chance of
your coming across anything, and it is very hot for
such hard work. But please yourselves; I don't wish
to prevent you. A friend of mine did once hit upon
a valuable coin in a place somewhat like this. His
dog was scratching a hole; he amused himself with
helping him; and about a foot and a half down he
found this coin, which turned out to be both very
ancient and very rare."

"Then I am sure we will have a look," said Jack.
"I have not dragged this lumbering old pickaxe up
here for nothing. Come on, boys; who knows what
luck we may have?"

They all gathered round, and, amidst much laughter, Jack set bravely to work. Alice grew so excited that the boys offered her the pickaxe to dig for herself. The elders seated themselves on some stones near, and awaited the result. About twenty minutes had elapsed—the boys having taken it by turns to dig—when a cry from Victor drew every one to the spot. He had come upon something very hard. He worked carefully now, and in a few minutes went down upon his hands and knees, and drew out a broken earthenware pitcher.

" Hurrah! hurrah!" cried the boys.

" It must be very old," called out one.

" How curious the handle is!" said another.

" Here, let me see it," said Mr. Merton—who was the best informed of the party on such subjects— taking it from Jack's hand.

He examined it with much attention; and handing it on to Mr. Armstrong, he said to Jack, with a peculiar expression on his face, as if he were speaking of a matter of the utmost importance: " It is not such a *very* strange thing to come across a pitcher in a courtyard, especially near a well. That pitcher has been used, though, rather later than the date of this building. But I should advise you to search further; you seem to be fortunate, and may make some more discoveries."

Meanwhile Tom had been digging away, and now rushed up with two copper pieces of money in his hand.

"Still more extraordinary!" said Mr. Merton, to whom they were given for inspection. "Ahem! ahem!—really quite strange! And I see here the remains of a Latin inscription, which will, of course, prove their age. Ahem! ahem! Jack, will you kindly wipe the dirt off them a little? Ahem!"

"My dear husband," interrupted Mrs. Merton, "you have taken cold. How you are coughing!"

Mr. Merton did not answer his wife with more than a look, but taking the coins from Jack again, asked what was to be done with them.

"Alice has not examined them yet, and she is an authority. Besides, but for her we never should have been lucky enough to find them.—Here, Alice, come and take the precious things. What, now, should you think would be their date?"

Alice's face was pale with excitement, and her hands trembled as she received the coins.

"I think they must be *very* ancient, father; don't you?" she said, after dead silence had reigned at least three minutes.

Her little speech was received with yells of laughter. She looked up then, and perceived that she had been taken in.

"Ha! ha! so the clever young lady does not know the date of old Ned Harris's beer-jug?"

"A penny twenty years old is *very* ancient."

"What will you sell it for?"

"Very ancient indeed."

Alice bit her lips, and turned to her parents and Mr. and Mrs. Armstrong; but they were laughing as merrily as the juveniles. Only Elsie looked distressed at the turn affairs had taken.

"It is wicked of you—it is unkind, cruel to trick me so!" cried out poor Alice. And then when Tom called out to know if she had seen the man who had locked her in the tower, she could bear it no longer, but burst into a passion of tears; and crying out that they were disgusting, horrible boys, she hated them every one, she allowed Elsie to take her arm, and try to drag her away.

Mr. Merton, however, now advanced, and told Alice not to be a silly child, but to dry her eyes and treat the matter as a good joke, instead of losing her temper and making all her friends feel uncomfortable.

The rest of the party then set off to continue their rambles, leaving Alice, Elsie, Georgie, and Conrad standing together. Georgie was so surprised to see Alice put out in this way that she stayed behind—

though she would much have liked to have joined the boys—to ask forgiveness for the share she had taken in the trick.

"Do forgive me, Allie dear. Indeed, I did not know that you would mind so much."

"I will never forgive you, Georgina; you are a nasty, horrid girl!" sobbed out Alice. "I will never love you again—no, never!"

Georgie's nature was an impulsive one. She was eager to make peace a minute ago; but now her sister's unkind words acted like cold water, and she answered carelessly: "Well, then, don't; I don't care. And I wouldn't be such a cry-baby as you for all the world.—Come on, Con; we won't stay here with a cry-baby." And putting her arm round him, she led him away.

Alice and Elsie were now left to their own devices; and no one being near, Alice allowed her friend to wipe away her tears, whilst she contented herself with abusing every one, and grumbling to her heart's content.

Meanwhile Georgie and Con went off together, for they knew not in which direction the boys had gone; and as they did not care to join the elders, they amused themselves with climbing the walls, though many a time they barely escaped severe tumbles.

Some parts of the old castle were in tolerable preservation, especially over the chapel, where there was an upper chamber carpeted with grass and ornamented with two elder-berry trees. The twins decided they would get up there; though it was really a somewhat dangerous undertaking, for some of the stones were loose, and every now and then they had to make desperate efforts not to lose their footing. However, they could both climb well; and in the end, after a great deal of exertion, they reached the chamber in safety. The sun was still powerful; so, as they felt rather weary, they sat down to rest for about quarter of an hour before they attempted to climb to the top of the chapel. As soon as they felt refreshed they scrambled up, and then commenced the perilous exploit of walking round the wall. Many a person in their position would have turned giddy and fallen; but not even Conrad experienced this sensation, and both enjoyed themselves immensely.

Suddenly Georgie espied an old jack-daw's nest in a crevice in the wall a few feet below where she was standing. "Don't you see it, Con, down there? I think I must have a try to get it."

"You had better not, Geo; you have never climbed down there before, and you don't want to sprain your ankle again."

There was Elsie!

"Nonsense, you silly boy; it is as easy as A B C. You wait here; or, no, you get down this other side into the chapel, and go and see after that sulky Alice. Just find out if she is still in the dumps. Give her my compliments, and say I hope she is better."

"Very well, Geo; but do take care of yourself."

"All right, old boy. But now make haste down, for the time is going."

Georgie watched Con descend and start off on his search in obedience to her orders; and then she began herself to climb down to the spot where she had seen the nest. She could not but be surprised to find how much easier the descent was than she had anticipated. Convenient resting-places seemed to appear for hands and feet just when she required them; and consequently in a very short space of time she had reached the hole.

She looked in. What was it she saw that astonished her so much that she nearly fell, though a second before she had been resting in perfect security? There must be something very peculiar about that little crevice, or the old jack-daw's nest. She looks in again; and this time she makes a longer inspection, which seems to satisfy her. But she does not take the nest which she had come to fetch, and

commences at once to climb up again to the top of
the chapel. Thence she rapidly descends into the
upper chamber, and then into the chapel itself. She
sets off at a run, and is soon out of sight.

After the lapse of a few minutes she appears again,
accompanied by Mr. Merton and Jack Armstrong.
She leads them into the chapel, and points out the
spot where was the old nest. Mr. Merton shakes his
head; but Jack climbs up, as Georgie had done, and
is soon gazing intently into the crevice. We will
look in over his shoulder. This crevice is the window
of a small dark room; and in it are a broken table,
a stool, and a large old chest. So much can be dis-
tinguished in the dimness. The crevice was too
narrow for any one to get through; where, then, was
the entrance?

Jack came down and reported what he had seen
to Mr. Merton. "I cannot make out how a fellow
can get in," said he. "It must be one of those secret
rooms built in the wall; and by the look of the
furniture some one must have lived there not so
very many years ago."

"I should think," said Mr. Merton, "that the wisest
plan would be to go to Ned Harris and ask him if
he knows anything of it. If any one can tell us, he
ought to be able to."

" Of course he ought," answered Jack ; and away he and Georgie started to the old man's cottage. Luckily they met him half way, and began eagerly questioning him ; but he was as much astonished as they had been, and declared " he had never heard either his father or his grandfather tell of such a place." He came back with them, and looked up at the crevice from below.

" Can you guess at all where the entrance can be, Harris ?" asked Mr. Merton.

" Indeed no, sir ; that I can't. It seems to be in the wall ; but there is no door nor any staircase about that side of the chapel that I ever knew of."

Georgie was much disappointed, as she had hoped to follow out her discovery. Presently the old man, who had been gazing intently at the wall, said to Mr. Merton,—

" Do you think, sir, it would be possible for the entrance to be anywhere in the dungeons ? Some of them lie underneath the chapel."

" That is not a bad idea, Harris, and I should not be surprised if you are right. Have you any candles ? because I would willingly explore down there."

" Yes, sir ; I was just coming up to say I would go through them, if any of your party liked, and was

bringing a supply of candles with me, when I met
the young lady and young gentleman."

"Oh, very well; then we will go at once."

"Thank you, father, oh, thank you so much!"
cried out Georgie, overjoyed; "but would you mind
waiting a minute whilst I call Connie, he wanted so
much to see them,—and Alice and Elsie too?"

"You may go after them if you like," said her
father; "but Alice scarcely deserves to be allowed to
go, after her silly behaviour just now."

Georgie was gone already, and did not hear the last
part of the sentence. Away she flew, shouting at the
top of her voice,—

'Con, Alice, Elsie; quick, come! We are going to
the dungeons. Con, Alice; quick, quick!"

In a very few minutes she came upon Conrad, who
told her Alice was quite close; so she hastened to tell
her to come, having in her excitement quite forgotten
all about their little quarrel. The friends were together as usual, and Alice was merry enough; but
the sight of her sister seemed to bring all her troubles
back, and in consequence she answered sulkily that
she did not care to come.

"Father said you were to," said Georgie. —"Don't
you care to see them, Elsie? I have made a wonderful discovery—a secret room in the wall, and we are

going to hunt for the entrance to it in the dungeons
Father is waiting, so come on."

"I come when I choose to," replied Alice.

"Oh, very well, Crosspatch; you will lose all the
fun, and make Elsie lose it too. I shan't wait for you;
so we will make haste, Con, and not keep father."

Off the twins ran, hand in hand; and soon they
were prepared, with their candles ready lighted, to
commence the investigation. Just as they were about
to descend, however, Alice and Elsie rushed up, and
begged to be allowed to come too. Mr. Merton ac-
ceded to their request; Harris provided them with
candles, and at last the party started. It was dreadfully dark and cold in the dungeons. Harris led the
way, with Mr. Merton by his side, and the young
people had orders to follow them closely.

"Do you know all the turnings and twistings,
Harris?" asked Jack Armstrong at last, after they
had wandered through dungeon after dungeon, and
had examined numerous old rusty chains and such
like things.

"Oh no, young sir; I nor any one living does, that
I know of; there are such a lot of them, you see, sir.
Now, these large ones we are coming to are supposed
to lie under the chapel, so if there is an entrance it
must be in one or other of these cells."

All the party began now to examine the damp, mouldy walls, very carefully. Alice and Elsie did not like this part at all, and found it rather irksome.

"Is it not cold here?" said Elsie at length.

"Dreadfully!" replied Alice. "I think this is the most horrible dungeon of all. I wish father would not stay here so awfully long; he will never find that stupid place; and I don't see why we should be frozen for Georgie's pleasure. I propose we go up again; I hate this dark, dismal place."

"But suppose we lose ourselves!" said Elsie. "I should like to go up into daylight again most certainly, but I should not at all like to lose myself."

"Don't be silly, Elsie, and come. Father is not looking this way now."

All the same Mr. Merton heard the hollow sound of their foot-steps, when they began to move, and instantly called to them to come back again.

"Please, father, cannot we go up? We don't like being down here, it is so cold and horrid."

"What! you don't care to assist us in our search? Well, then, you may go.—Harris, just show them the way out; we will wait here for you."

Harris accordingly conducted them to the foot of the steps that would take them back to the fresh air; and they were half way up, when Elsie discovered she had lost her locket, a very pretty one that Mr. Armstrong had given her on her last birthday.

"I know I had it on when we went down," said she. "I remember feeling it, to see if it were safe. Oh, Alice, we must go down again; do you mind coming?"

"Indeed I do mind very much," said Alice most ungraciously; "but of course you cannot go alone. How stupid you were to lose it!"

"Oh, please don't come, dear Alice, if you don't want to. I daresay I shall find it in a few minutes. You shall not come, really you shan't;" and blowing out her friend's candle, the little girl hurried down the steps, and soon found herself alone in the dungeons. Alice did not attempt to follow her; and, well pleased at having escaped going down a second time into these dismal abodes, she wandered away by herself, and left Elsie to her fate!

CHAPTER VII

MEANWHILE Mr. Merton and Harris examined most carefully every spot which
they thought to be at all likely to lead up
to the secret room; but their search was
in vain,—not a trace of a door, a passage,
or a staircase could they discover. Up
and down they looked, into dark, damp corners; in
fact, they scarcely passed over a square foot of those
dungeons, which Harris informed them lay beneath
the chapel, without subjecting it to the strictest investigation.

The whole party were much disappointed when at
last they turned their steps homewards, and were
more than ever at a loss in respect to the whereabouts
of the entrance they sought for. It seemed so strange
when once more they came into daylight; they had
to shade their eyes with their hands; the sun seemed
to dazzle them after the gloomy light below.

"I am really very sorry, Georgie; but I don't know what more we can do," said Mr. Merton.

"Nor I, father. It is vexing, I own; but then it can't be helped, and we have had all the fun of going down into the dungeons. I am awfully glad I don't live in the days when people were shut up in places like that. It must almost have been like being buried alive."

"So it must, my dear. No one can tell what agonies the poor wretches confined there must have endured. It is, indeed, a blessing to our country that such iniquities have been done away with."

"Is it not nearly five o'clock, Mr. Merton?" asked Jack Armstrong presently, his own watch being, as was usually the case in holiday-time, at the watch-maker's to be repaired.

"Yes, indeed; it is past; it is going on for six o'clock. Tea was to be ready at five.—Aren't you hungry, Con? I feel starving."

"Well, here we are, and here is tea ready!" sang out Georgie, as they approached a snug corner where a kettle was boiling, gipsy-fashion, on three rickety sticks, and an inviting-looking meal was ready prepared. Harris busied himself with finding some other sticks for the kettle, and the whole party were soon engaged in partaking of the good things, when suddenly Tom said,—

"I say, where's Elsie? She is not here."

No one had noticed her absence till then; now all felt disturbed.

"Why, Alice," said Mr. Merton, "you must know where she left you; you went out of the dungeons together."

"Yes, father; but—"

"Speak out, child; is anything the matter?"

Mr. Merton spoke peremptorily, and Alice, bursting into tears, confessed how Elsie had gone back after her locket.

"Alice, you knew this, and never mentioned it all this time!" said her father, in a tone of bitter reproach. Mr. and Mrs. Armstrong, as in fact were all the party, felt extremely alarmed for the safety of the missing one. Harris was at once summoned, fresh candles fetched, and then he, Mr. Armstrong, Mr. Merton, Jack, and Victor set forth to search. Georgie begged hard to come, and at the last moment Mr. Merton consented to take her, thinking her quick eyes and courageous, active spirit, might prove useful. They walked quickly, and soon reached the dungeons. Harris led the way; the rest followed, shouting at intervals. They went through every step of the way they had gone over that afternoon, but not a sign of Elsie was to be seen! In dismal cells, and damp, dark corners, up and down the narrow passages, they wandered, shouting, "Elsie! Elsie!" but no voice answered theirs; and when at last old Harris declared he had taken them over all the parts he knew, their hearts began to beat quickly, and they dreaded what might be.

"I have heard tell, sir," said their guide, "that there are some pits down in the lowest dungeons. It may be that perhaps the poor young lady has fallen down one of them."

This information was not likely to raise their hopes, but they continued their search with redoubled energy, and looked out carefully for any of those horrible pits. Their candles were already half burnt away, and they all felt prepared for any horror that might be coming.

"My poor little girl!" said Mr. Armstrong at last. "I cannot go back and tell her mother that she is lost to us, and in this wretched place."

"I heard Mrs. Armstrong say," here put in Georgie, "that if we did not return in an hour, she should come and look for Elsie herself."

"I heard her say so too," added Jack. "I trust she won't be so mad though, for this is no place for her."

The party were now all standing still, looking pale

and anxious as the flickering light of the candles shone upon their faces.

"Indeed no," said the unhappy father; "but she might take it into her head, and there is no one could stop her doing anything she thought could help one of her children, especially in such a case as this. Could not some one go back and tell her on no account to venture, and that we shall search on till we find some trace."

"I will go, if you like," said Georgie. "I can see the opening down at the end of that long passage."

"God bless you, my dear; and may He give me back my child," murmured Mr. Armstrong, as Georgie turned down the long passage which led to the entrance. They all felt it impossible that she could miss the path, so they went onwards to continue their search. When Georgie had gone about half way she suddenly perceived something white lying on the ground in a narrow passage on her right. She went up to it, took it into her hand, and discovered it to be a pocket-handkerchief. She looked at the name in the corner; it was "Elsie Armstrong." Georgie now examined the damp floor to see if she could there discover anything more that would assist them in the search. She could not be mistaken. She

held the candle lower—yes, there were decided marks
of footsteps about the right size, and they were going
onwards.   Forgetful of all else in the excitement of
the moment, she continued to follow them.   They
now turned to the left, and were distinctly visible in
a very narrow passage, so small that only one person
could pass through at a time.   With the greatest
care Georgie was enabled to distinguish the foot-
prints as she pressed on.   Suddenly she rushed forward with a low cry, for there lay a half-burnt
candle, and close beside it was the missing locket,
the cause of all this trouble.   Eagerly Georgie
snatched up both candle and locket, and stuffed them
into her pocket, and then she hastened on.   Somehow the idea of returning to inform the other
searchers never entered her mind.   "Poor Elsie!
fancy her being in this awful place with no candle!
I must and will find her."   This was her thought,
this was her determination.   She raised her candle
and surveyed the passage—it seemed to be endless;
but she boldly pressed onwards in the traces of the
footsteps.   At last it seemed to her that the floor
was ascending—she was sure of it—she was no
longer walking on a level surface; she was mount-
ing—but whither?   Once more she stood still and
held up her candle; she had reached the end of the

passage, and now stood with one foot resting on the
first step of a narrow stone staircase. On this she
could distinguish no traces ; but having carefully
examined the walls on either side, she soon saw there
was no other outlet, so the only thing for her to do
was to mount without delay. She commenced the
ascent. The staircase was a winding one, and poor
Georgie almost thought it would never end. On and
on she climbed. "Oh dear, I *am* tired," she said to
herself, but still she toiled upwards. Once she
stopped to light the half candle she had picked up.
"I was uncommonly lucky to find this," she thought,
"or I should have been left in the dark like Elsie.
I wonder where in the world this staircase can lead
to." Suddenly she remembered the secret room ;—
could this be the way up to it? The idea put fresh
life into her; and the next turn of the staircase
revealed a sight she never afterwards forgot; such a
feeling of joy came over her that she felt nearly
choked by it. There was Elsie seated, all crouched
together, her head, with its pretty curly locks, resting on a dirty, damp step; she was sleeping, but the
tears were trickling down her pale face, whilst her
fingers worked nervously with the elastic of her hat,
which she held fast in both hands. Georgie hastened up to her, crying out,—

"Elsie, Elsie—wake up! wake up! I am come to save you. It will be all right now."

The young girl raised herself with an effort, looked at Georgie earnestly, and then said in a low voice,—"Is it really you, Georgie Merton? are you alive?"

"Alive! yes, yes, you dear; of course I am. How did you come to lose yourself, you poor creature? Take care of the candle; you can kiss me presently, you know. Now we must be hurrying on."

"What had we better do?" asked Elsie, looking quite happy again. "Do you know, Georgie, I thought I should never be found, and that I should be left here and be starved to death. I never felt so miserable in all my life."

"Well, never mind; 'tis come right at last. We must get upstairs quickly though, or the candle will be burned out. Mine is gone; this is yours which I picked up.

"Ah, yes," said Elsie, as she followed Georgie up the staircase, "I slipped my foot and fell down. My candle went out, and I couldn't find it again, so that was lost, and my poor locket, which I had just found, and had tight in my hand. I tried to find the way out, but could not, and instead came on up here, and at last I felt so tired and so frightened that

I could do nothing but cry; and then I sat down, and I think I went to sleep."

"Yes, you were sleeping when I found you. And good news for you, Elsie, I picked up your locket, and have got it quite safe in my pocket."

"Oh, thank you, Georgie; but where do you think this staircase can lead to? It seems never-ending, and my legs they do ache so."

"Mine do awfully too. I expect this staircase leads into the secret room I discovered in the chapel wall," answered Georgie, "and I am not sure, but I think this must be nearly the top. Hurrah! here we are, and just in time too, for my candle is burned out. I declare, this is the very room I peered into!"

The two girls now stood in the tiny chamber, glanced round it, and then hurried to the opening which formed the window.

"Georgie, this is all very well, it is not dark here like it is down in the dungeons, but I don't a bit see how we are to squeeze out through here, and I would not at all like to stay all night." Elsie looked ready to cry again, and Georgie too looked rather disturbed.

"Oh, bother," she said, "I never thought of that, and we can't go down, for our candles are all gone. I will shout, and perhaps some one may hear us. I wish I could push out one of these stones, and then we could easily manage to get out. Come and try, Elsie." But the strength of the two young captives had no power to stir the massive stone, so they set to work to shout and cry for help at the top of their voices.

In the meantime, the party in the dungeons continued their search in vain, and about half an hour after Georgie's departure they were forced to come up in order to fetch more candles from Harris's cottage. They found the rest anxiously awaiting their arrival at the entrance, and when they had to report their bad news, Mrs. Armstrong's distress was unbounded. She had much wished to descend, but Mrs. Merton would not hear of her doing such a thing.

"Surely Georgie told you not to come?" said Mr. Merton nervously, fearful that perhaps she too had lost her way. Before he could receive an answer every one was startled by loud cries of "Help! help!" which sounded through the stillness of the evening air.

"That is Georgie's voice," said one.

"No, 'twas Elsie's," said another.

The whole party rushed forward and soon reached the chapel, from whose neighbourhood the calls had proceeded. Tom was first.

"There they are!" he said. "Don't you see a handkerchief moving about in that crevice up there?"

"Why, that's the secret room!" ejaculated Mr. Merton; "how did they ever get there? and how in the world are they ever to be got out?"

"Are you both safe?" shouted Mr. Armstrong.

"Yes, all right!" came down the answer.

Jack had by this time reached the upper chamber, and in a few minutes was scrambling up to the crevice. It was hard work going up this way, but he was surefooted, and soon his hands were resting in the opening, and his feet perched on two projecting stones.

"How did you come up here?" he asked breathlessly.

"From the dungeons, by an awful long steep staircase," was the reply of both girls; whilst Georgie added, "I found Elsie half way up; her candle had gone out, and she was fast asleep."

"Well, I am sure 'tis a mercy you are safe; but how do you propose to get out, if you please?"

"We don't know," said Georgie. "If one of these stones could be pushed out, we could easily climb down; if not, I suppose we must go back by those horrid dungeons again, and we can't do that without some more candles anyhow."

"I don't mean you to do it either, if I can help it,'

said Jack, "for it strikes me we have had quite
enough of dungeons for one day. Keep up your
courage, girls, and we will soon have you out. I
must go down now." When he reached the lookers-
on below, and had reported that the youthful
prisoners were unharmed and perfectly safe, but that
there was no entrance except from the dungeons, he
added, "I should think, though, that if we had a good
strong ladder, we might loosen one of those stones in
the opening with a crow-bar, and then the girls could
come down that way."

"You are quite right, Jack, my boy," said Mr.
Armstrong.—"Harris, do you possess such things as
a ladder and a crow-bar?"

"Yes, sir; but I don't see how you are going to get
a ladder anywhere that will reach right up there.
Mine is only about eight feet long."

"That will do splendidly," said Mr. Merton; "we
can haul it up into the upper chamber and climb
from there. Please get it, Harris, as quickly as you
can.—One of you boys had better go and help him
to bring it up."

In about quarter of an hour the ladder arrived,
and, by means of a rope, was safely dragged up into
the chamber by Mr. Merton and Jack, whilst the
others assisted by pushing from below. At last it

was firmly fixed, and then Mr. Merton holding it
securely, Jack mounted, crow-bar in hand. The job
was a tedious one, but at last patient perseverance
was rewarded; and the great stone, which Jack had
been working at, became so loose that he could move
it with his hands quite easily.

"Get away, right outside the chapel," he shouted
out to his friends below. "I am going to throw this
stone down."

"Steady, Jack, for pity's sake be careful," said Mr.
Merton, as the young fellow dragged the stone to the
edge and allowed it to roll over.

"Now girls, do you think you can squeeze through
there?" asked he, after cleaning away some of the
rubbish that stuffed up the hole.

"Oh yes," said they both.

"Then listen. You had better not come down by
this ladder, which is not particularly firm just now.
I fancy you will be much safer if you drop down into
our arms. Father or Mr. Merton could catch you
easily."

"Very well; we don't mind either way if we only
get out," answered Georgie. "Elsie had better go
first; she is the eldest prisoner."

"All right; but before you come down just take a
peep into that chest."

"Oh, there is nothing there," she replied. "I have looked in already; it is empty, dreadfully dirty, and so rotten."

Jack descended, moved aside the ladder, and stood with his father and Mr. Merton in the grass-carpeted chamber below. Mr. Merton, being a taller, stronger man than Mr. Armstrong, volunteered to receive the children in his arms as they dropped down. Elsie scrambled out first; Georgie assisted her as best she could, and then she clung on to the ledge with her hands.

"Now, then, Elsie, are you ready? Don't be afraid; I will catch you safely enough. One—two—three—drop!"

In a second, it seemed, the little girl was in his arms. Georgie came down next, and then they all descended into the chapel, where they were joyfully welcomed by the rest of the party. The anxiety Alice had undergone had quite subdued her bad temper, and she was now very humble and shame-faced.

After a few minutes' chatter, Mrs. Merton proposed that a second edition of tea would be rather nice, after which they must start off home, as it was now nearly eight o'clock. Immediately it seemed to occur to all that they felt uncommonly hungry, though

no one had really any occasion to be so, as they had
well-nigh finished a most substantial tea when Elsie
was missed, except the lost one herself, who had
tasted nothing since dinner. The consequence was
that the fire was rekindled, some more tea made, and
before they departed they had devoured everything
they could lay their fingers on, except the cups and
plates themselves, which Mrs. Merton suggested they
had better leave for a future meal!

It was a beautiful summer evening, and the cool air
was most enjoyable after the heat and labours of the
day. A handsome present was made to old Harris
for all his extra trouble, and shortly before nine the
party were quietly floating down the river homewards. Presently the boys took the oars, and it was
not long before they reached the rectory lawn; and
there, bidding each other farewell, the two families
separated, having thoroughly enjoyed their expedition, notwithstanding the fright they had had. Alice
was still very silent, and felt thoroughly ashamed of
the manner in which she had behaved. She was, in
fact, the only one who felt uncomfortable as the
children followed their parents into Merton House.
She was hastening upstairs, having hurriedly bid her
father and mother good-night, when Mrs. Merton
called her back, and said, quietly,—

"I am coming up in a few minutes, Alice, as I am tired, and I should like to see you in my dressing-room before you go to bed."

Quarter of an hour later, the mother and daughter were together. Mrs. Merton talked to her very gently about giving way to such foolish temper as she had done that day, representing to her that it would have been far better to have taken the little joke in good part, and to have joined in the laugh over it.

"You see, dear Alice, it was only done in fun; no harm was intended, and you made every one feel quite uncomfortable by bursting out crying and going on in the silly way you did. It distressed me much to see you had so little command over yourself."

"I am very sorry," murmured Alice; "indeed I am, dear mother. I see now how wrong I was."

"Another thing too, my child, I must speak to you about. How was it you did not mention a word about Elsie before you were questioned? The consequences might have been most dreadful had not Georgie been so fortunate as to discover that pocket-handkerchief, and bravely pressed onwards. It was indeed a great mercy, and we ought all to be most thankful for it. How was it Elsie came to return to the dungeons alone?"

Alice was silent.

"You must answer me, Alice," said Mrs. Merton.

"She asked me to go back with her, but I was cross, and did not want to go down into the horrible place again, so she went alone; and then, when she did not come back, I was afraid to say anything, though I longed to speak out, because I thought if she were lost down there it would be almost as if I had killed her by letting her go back by herself; and then I should be a—a—murderess!"

The last words were uttered very low; but the mother heard them, and, taking one of Alice's hands in hers, she said, very earnestly,—

"My child, do you know that you did wrong, very wrong. You thought only of yourself, not of your friend, and your selfishness might have cost her her life. Oh, Alice darling, you must try to overcome this fault of yours; don't live only for yourself, but think of those around you."

Alice was now crying very softly, and she promised her mother again and again that she would try to do better in future.

"Good-night, dear; I trust the fright you have had to-day you will never forget, and that it will be a lesson to you."

The mother and child then embraced each other with great tenderness, and separated for the night.

CHAPTER VIII.

THE SEA-SIDE.

T was determined, after much consultation, that the last fortnight of the holidays should be spent by the younger members of the Merton family, under the charge of Mrs. Merton and old nurse, at the sea-side, and the place fixed upon was Eastcliff. The truth was that Georgie, although she considered herself perfectly recovered from her sprained ankle and the illness that attended it, was subject at times to fits of languor and weakness so foreign to her nature that the doctor thought a blow of sea air would do her a world of good. The announcement was hailed with great delight. Tom and Twig had never been to the sea before, and the elder ones had not been for many years. Norman was to leave home at the same time with his friend and tutor, Mr. Hazlewood, and under his care make a short tour in Switzerland; whilst Mr. Merton and Lily were to visit Miss Merton at Mure Hill. Norman was the first to set out on his travels, charmed at the prospect before him.

The following day was fixed for the departure to Eastcliff, and proved to be all that could be desired in respect to the weather. The long journey ended at last, and the first thing to be done was to convey the party to their lodging, where they were welcomed by a fat old landlady, with bright green ribbons, and yellow roses in her cap. After tea, the evening being lovely and the tide in, nothing would do but that the children should first all go into the town to invest in baskets for the elder, and spades and buckets for the younger ones, and thence proceed to the beach, where Tom and Twig immediately ran into the sea, and got their boots thoroughly soaked through. Nurse scolded in vain, for no one could help laughing at the intense gravity with which Twig said,—

"I's so sorry, nursie; but me did not know the big sea would tum to wet me. Me did not know the big sea was wet; 'deed nursie, dear."

They did not remain out very long; for after the first excitement was over, they all discovered how tired and sleepy they were, and were not sorry to return home and go straight to bed. Two or three days passed by in undisturbed enjoyment. Georgie

had no fits of weakness; her spirits were always at
their old pitch, and quite a pink tinge of colour was
visible on her cheeks. During this time the Mertons
made acquaintance with three other children, who
usually went down to play on the beach at the same
hours as themselves. Their name was Hamilton, and
they only lived a few doors off, so it was not long
before the two families became quite intimate. The
eldest of these new friends was a handsome, good-
tempered boy of twelve, called Harry. Maud, who
came next, was ten, and seemed a very pleasant little
girl; whilst Charlie, the youngest, was five, and
amused every one by the immense care he took of
Twig, who was only a year younger.

Donkey rides were esteemed a great treat, and
though the Mertons found donkeys were not nearly
so nice as their own ponies at home, still they
thoroughly enjoyed the fun of being jolted about.

One day at dinner Mrs. Merton said, "I have a
piece of good news for you, children; can you guess
what it is?"

Many and strange were the guesses they made,
until at last Georgie said,—

"Mother, is it that we are to go out in a boat?"

"Right, Georgie," was the answer; and then such
shrieks of delight arose from them all, that Mrs,

Merton was forced to wait a minute or two before she went on. "Captain Hamilton has been here this morning, and has invited us to join him. Mrs. Hamilton and the children are going, so I think we shall be a merry party."

About three o'clock the two families went down together to the beach, where they found an old sailor and the boat in readiness. They soon started; the sea was as calm as a duck-pond, and they anticipated a most delightful trip. Conrad was sitting in the stern, and presently grew very restless; whilst those near him heard him say, half to himself and half to them,—

"Oh, I don't like it, I don't like it! I know we shall be upset." But no one took any notice of his fears.

After going a little way out, the sail was hoisted; and then the old sailor, speaking to him for the first time, said good-naturedly,—

"Perhaps, young master, you will like sailing better than rowing."

The sail, however, made matters worse, for a slight breeze catching it, the boat went somewhat on one side; and Conrad, thinking they were immediately going to be drowned, commenced screaming loudly. Mrs. Merton tried soothing and scolding without

effect, and Captain and Mrs. Hamilton did the same.
He would persist in behaving in this babyish fashion,
so at last Mrs. Merton said,—

"Well, Conrad, I am quite ashamed of you; and
as I cannot allow every one's pleasure to be spoiled
by a silly, naughty boy, who believes his friends
would willingly take him into danger, Captain
Hamilton, will you kindly order Richards to take us
back to shore? We will leave Conrad there, and go
on our trip without this unpleasant noise."

The moment Con heard this he seemed quite contented, and ceased screaming. In a very short time
he was landed, and placed under the charge of
nurse, who had been enjoying the sunshine on the
beach, and amusing herself with watching the boat
as it sped on its way over the smooth sea.

He did not feel quite happy, though, when his
mother said aloud, so that every one heard,—

"Take Master Conrad home, nurse, at once, and
put him to bed; that is the only proper place for
naughty, babyish boys."

At first the pleasure of the children was somewhat
marred by the thought of Conrad's disgrace, but they
soon forgot their trouble; and when Harry Hamilton
produced a fishing-line from his pocket, and declared
his intention of catching a number of fish, the greatest

excitement prevailed. Nothing would do but that they must all have lines too. Luckily, Harry had a small box of hooks, and amongst them they had sufficient string for the purpose. The hooks were speedily baited with bread, and soon all were engaged in the new amusement. Twig, who was being held fast by his mother lest he should tumble overboard, was the first to be successful, and greatly delighted was he, when, with Mrs. Merton's assistance, he managed to draw into the boat a small fish, which old Richards soon killed with a blow on its head. Among them the children caught nine, and excessively proud they felt. Coming home, the sail was obliged to be taken down, and the oars once more put into requisition. Tom and Georgie took an oar between them for a while; but rowing was such hard work, and the oars were so heavy, that they felt quite thankful when Maud and Harry Hamilton offered to relieve them.

Whilst the young folks had been thus amusing themselves, the elders of the party had made arrangements for a picnic to Crawford Bay on the following Thursday, which was Tom's birthday. It was agreed that the plan should be kept a secret until the day came, in order that it might be a pleasant surprise both to Tom and his companions. Birthdays were regularly kept in the Merton family, and the children had always much pleasure beforehand in preparing numerous little presents. When Tom came down to breakfast on the eventful morning, which, by the way, he did in unusually good time, a most wonderful collection of queerly-shaped parcels were placed in a high pile where his breakfast-plate should have been. When he opened them, he seemed to find there everything he most wanted. There was a long letter and a splendid large wheel-barrow from his father, a nice box of water-colours from his mother, a long letter and photograph from Norman, a new whip from Lily, a big knife with two blades from Georgie, a pen and pencil-case from Con, a popgun with a double spring from Alice, and a large box of chocolate from Twig, whilst nurse had added as her share a big bag of barley-sugar. Tom's delight knew no bounds; he ran from one person to another, displaying his presents and uttering his rather noisy thanks. Breakfast certainly was longer than usual that day, but it was over at last, and then Mrs. Merton told the children she had invited the Hamiltons to spend the day with them. Presently the whole Hamilton family arrived—father, mother, Harry, Maud, and little Charlie. The first thing to be done, of course, was to have a fresh show-off of the presents, to which

Harry added another in the shape of a box of capital crackers. Then Mrs. Merton said,—

"Now, young people, there is such a treat in store for you; make haste and get ready, for we are going to spend the day at Crawford Bay."

The news was hailed with screams of delight, and not very long after the whole party were safely packed in a large brake, and fast proceeding on their way.

Just as they were going to start, who should appear, to their immense surprise, but Mr. Merton! It seemed that he had been obliged to come on business to a small town close by the day before, and had then determined he would astonish them by paying them a flying visit before he returned to Mure Hill. As might be supposed, nothing would do now but that he should accompany them on their excursion; so room was made for him in the carriage, and he was soon chatting away with Captain and Mrs. Hamilton as if he had known them for years.

Crawford Bay was about five miles distant from Eastcliff. It was a wild, romantic spot, with steep cliffs and rugged rocks stretching out far into the sea. The tide was out when the brake deposited its joyous burden and the big hampers of good things. Having discovered a beautiful sheltered nook for the elders, and left the hampers, wraps, and such like things under nurse's care, the younger members of the party set off to clamber about and enjoy themselves. They were all arrayed in their oldest garments, so it mattered not in the least how dirty they made themselves, and many a tumble they had over the slimy sea-weed.

Even Charlie and Twig climbed easy rocks, though they were not allowed to go out of nurse's sight. They all felt quite sorry when the sound of a shrill whistle proclaimed to them that dinner was ready. With reluctant steps they returned, though they were bound to confess that the sea-breezes had made them hungry. In the centre of the table-cloth, which covered the rock that served them as a table was placed the birthday cake sent from Mure Hill the day before, where it had been specially made for the occasion by Miss Merton's old house-keeper. It was a most tempting-looking cake; and, in fact, such a cake as cannot be seen every day of the week. It was thickly frosted with white sugar, and over this snowy-looking ground were little pink, and brown, and white mice, running about in all directions, with great staring eyes, and long tails made of string. The mice themselves were made of sugar, and much fun there was, when the time came to partake of the cake, over the way the children, holding the wee creatures by their tails, bit off their heads.

Dinner being ended, away started the children again, after having been duly warned by their parents not to venture out too far, as the tide would soon be coming in. Georgie, always the most venturesome, had determined to climb over the rocks to a tiny bay she saw a short distance farther on. She asked who would accompany her, and Harry immediately volunteering, she told Conrad to devote himself to Maud, of whom he was very fond, as it would never do for a whole lot of them to go so far. The climb was hard work, but in the excitement that was forgotten. Georgie led the way; Harry followed. After about half an hour's clambering Georgie squatted herself on a rock, and waiting for her companion, said,—

"Here, Harry, come and sit down a bit; my legs are quite tired."

"I don't mind; and see, Georgie, isn't it lucky I have got my oldest suit on, for I am all in rags and tatters?"

After a short rest they both felt revived, and in another quarter of an hour they found themselves in the little bay. It was a lovely spot, and from it the view of Crawford Bay was perfect; but the children did not trouble themselves about that, as not a few minutes had elapsed before they discovered a large cave with a stream of fresh water running into it, and in the centre a pool, in which were the most beautiful anemones and sea-weeds. Overjoyed, they began to peer about more, and soon discovered that the floor of this delightful cave was composed almost entirely of lovely little shells of a kind they had never seen before. Down on their knees they went, and commenced filling their pockets and handkerchiefs with these treasures. Harry filled his cap as well, and, thus employed, they forgot how the time was slipping by.

" I say, Harry," said Georgie at last, " it must be getting late, I should think, and I suppose we ought to be seeing about going back. Won't the others be jealous of our discovery ? "

So saying, Georgie led the way out of the cave, and prepared to return, when suddenly raising her eyes, she perceived how very much the sea had advanced since they had set out.

" Just look, Harry ! Do you think we shall ever get over these rocks in time ? "

" Indeed I hope so, Georgie ; but do go on, and let us be as quick as possible."

On they hastened, but having something to carry

rather impeded their progress. They had reached
about half way, and could see their friends in
Crawford Bay beckoning to them to hurry on, when,
just as they were descending the slippery side of a
steep rock, Harry missed his footing, and fell, uttering a sharp scream. Georgie, who was a little in
advance as usual when his cry startled her, instantly
turned back, and was horrified to see poor Harry
lying motionless, with blood coming from his forehead. A moment more and she was at his side,
doing her utmost to revive him; for the boy had
knocked his head against a projecting piece of rock.
and the pain was so great that he had lost consciousness. Georgie, with trembling fingers wiped the
blood away, chafed his hands, and implored him to
look up. After a minute or two, which to her
seemed ages, Harry opened his eyes and asked,
" Where am I ? " in a faint tone.

Overjoyed to find he was not dead, Georgie raised
his head on to her lap, and asked him if he were
much hurt.

'Oh, my head hurts so ! " he answered.

" But, Harry, dear Harry, don't you think you
could get up ? We shall never get back, and the sea
is coming in so awfully fast. I will help you."

" I'll try, Georgie ; let me lean on you. You don't

mind, do you?" After a great effort the boy got upon his feet, but felt so giddy that he was forced to sit down again.

"Oh, Harry, do try once more; we shall never do it. Wait, though, a second, whilst I climb up and see if I can get any one to help you."

Georgie got on the top of the rock, and beckoned with her hand to the party, who were anxiously watching from Crawford Bay. She shook her head also, and gesticulated wildly, for she saw that the sea had advanced so far that to return in time with Harry in his almost helpless condition would be impossible. What then was to be done?

CHAPTER IX.

THE RESCUE.

GEORGIE descended the rock once more, and asked Harry, who was sitting crouched up, with his head, round which her neck-tie was bound, resting on his hand, if he felt any better.

"A little," said he, dolefully; "but when I try to move I feel so queer."

They were in a sort of hollow in the rocks, so that they could not see the sea.

"Harry," said Georgie, "don't be frightened; but, do you know, I am afraid we shan't be able to get back now, and we shall have to stay here all night!"

The boy turned paler than before, and, taking hold of Georgie's arm, raised himself up without speaking, and stared her in the face.

"'Tis true, Harry, quite; and another thing, we must try somehow to get up on that high rock; the sea will be coming in here presently. Just look; the spray is already coming over."

After no end of exertion on Georgie's part, and no end of suffering on Harry's, the two children at last found themselves seated close to each other on the top of a huge flat rock. It was the greatest relief to their friends to see them both there, as they had feared some dreadful accident had happened to Harry. The feeling, too, was the more terrible, as at first no way appeared possible in which they could assist them. A boat would be of no service, as it could not approach near enough; no one could climb to them. What was to be done? Must the children remain on the rock all night?

"I know," at last said Mr. Merton, "what we might do. We could haul them up over the cliff, if they would get a little further along to this side. See, the side of the cliff is fairly smooth, and with a strong rope and a strong arm I don't doubt but that we shall be able to get them up quite safely. What do you think, Hamilton?"

"That you are quite right, and that it is the only thing to be done, for we cannot leave them there till the tide goes down. I believe we are going to have a storm; and besides, I am sure my Harry is hurt. But where can we get a rope?"

The nearest house was a fisherman's hut, about quarter of an hour's walk distant, and thither the two gentlemen instantly went, having first sent the rest of the party home, except the two mothers, under the charge of nurse, with orders that the carriage was to return as soon as possible. The ladies remained on the beach, encouraging the children by waving their handkerchiefs, and making signs that help was coming. Meanwhile the rope was secured,—a good stout one; and accompanied by the fisherman, whom they were fortunate enough to find at home, the two anxious fathers set out on their way to the top of the cliff. It was a difficult, circuitous path, but half an hour's quick walking brought them to the spot.

During this time Georgie and Harry had been trying to raise each other's spirits; for, notwithstanding the signals, they could see no way in which help could reach them, and they naturally did not much like the idea of spending the night in this desolate spot. Poor Harry's head ached badly, and he could scarcely refrain from tears. He was lying down with his head resting on Georgie's lap, when she, smoothing back his hair, perceived some drops quivering on his lashes.

"Don't cry, Harry, don't cry! If it is very

horrible being here all the dark night, why, God will take care of us, just the same as if we were at home safe in bed; so cheer up, Harry, boy, and let us make the best of it. Is your head very bad now?"

"Yes," murmured he, stifling back a sob, "it aches horridly; and, O Georgie, I feel so ashamed of myself lying here like this, when I ought to be taking care of you, not you of me."

"Now, don't bother yourself about such nonsense as that. You are hurt and I am not, which makes all the difference; and besides, I would rather have you with me than be here alone, so you see you really are taking care of me in a way. I say, Harry, which would you rather be—a boy, or a girl?"

"A boy, of course!" said he with really quite a little laugh.

"So would I," said Georgie; "it is an awful bother being only a girl; one can't do half the things you boys can do."

"I should rather think you couldn't," said Harry in a louder tone, and in quite a superior manner.

Georgie was thus engaged in coaxing and comforting, when, O joy! she heard her father's voice calling to her close by. She looked around and then overhead, and called out in reply.

"Can you come a little more this way?" shouted

Mr. Merton. "We want to haul you up, and the cliff projects too much just here."

"Oh yes, father," she cried eagerly.—"Get up, Harry, and I will help you to climb along."

The hope of being rescued roused the weary child, and soon the pair were on the rock pointed out to them by their friends above. A few minutes more and Georgie had fastened the stout rope let down firmly round Harry's waist. She would not hear of going up first herself, and bidding him clutch tight hold of it with both hands, she shouted out, "All right!" and the rope began to move. Harry's heart beat quickly as he commenced his ascent, and he felt very frightened lest the rope might break, or any accident of that kind arise. At last his head appeared over the edge of the cliff; another minute and he was in his father's arms. He gazed a moment into his face, and then fainted away. The knowledge that once more he was safe was too much for him, and the pain in his poor head had made him weak. Captain Hamilton had brought some brandy with him, in case it might be needed, and a little of this soon revived him, so that, when Georgie reached his side, he was able to sit up and speak.

Georgie's ascent had been far more difficult than his, for during his, she, standing below, had been able to save him, by means of a thick piece of string fastened to the rope, from beating himself against the side of the cliff. The consequence was, the brave girl had been much knocked about; but she did not seem to mind, though she had received many a scrape and bruise from the rough edges of the rocks. Self was entirely forgotten; she seemed only to care about others.

"Oh, my darling!" said Mr. Merton as he clasped her to his breast, and thanked Heaven for giving her back to him,—"Oh, my darling, I never know how much I love you, how very dear you are to me, until there seems a chance of my losing you!" and the strong man's chest shook with a sob, and a scalding tear fell on his child's face. Georgie's arms stole softly round his neck, and she kissed him lovingly.

Mr. Merton's agitation only lasted a few seconds, when, recovering himself, he carefully wrapped a warm shawl round Georgie, and made her swallow a tiny drop of Captain Hamilton's brandy, as he feared her long exposure might be too much for her, when she had lately been so far from well. Georgie made a frightful face when she took it, and declared it was worse than the nastiest medicine.

The party now prepared to return to Crawford Bay. Georgie clung to her father's arm, and Harry was assisted by Captain Hamilton and the fisherman. He was feeling much better, and refused the fisherman's offer of carrying him right manfully. About an hour elapsed before they reached the beach, for the evening twilight was fast fading, and they had to pick their way carefully. How rejoiced the anxious mothers were to receive them, needs no telling; in fact, the two children ran a near chance, as they always afterwards positively declared, of being smothered by the kisses bestowed upon them. In a short time, however, they were once more comfortably packed into the carriage, and driving fast home.

None were unwilling to go to bed that night, and Georgie and Harry were both asleep almost before they were undressed. Next day Georgie felt rather stiff, and Harry's head ached a little; but these were the only bad results of their adventure at Tom's birthday picnic.

CHAPTER X.

ERY sorry were the Hamiltons and the Mertons to part when the time came for the holidays to end and the Mertons to return home; and many were the promises made, not only of writing to each other, but even of visiting each other on some future occasion. Norman had already returned from Switzerland, and Mr. Merton and Lily had quitted Mure Hill, so that now once again the family were reunited. They were very happy together, and little dreamt of the heavy sorrow that lay in store for them. The autumn days were cold and chilly; and as Twig was a delicate child, nurse used to have a fire lighted in the nursery long before fires were introduced into the other rooms. There was a high guard all round the fire-place; but Twig had a naughty trick of making long spills of paper and poking them in between the bars of this guard, to set them in a flame; and as soon as they began burning he was charmed, for, like many other little children, he did not realize the danger of playing with fire. Nurse had often punished him for doing so; and many a time Twig had spent ten minutes in the corner, or been placed with a handkerchief tied over his eyes on a high chair. He always promised he would never disobey again, but he invariably forgot his good resolutions when next an opportunity offered for indulging in the forbidden amusement.

One day nurse was called away from the nursery for a few minutes, and left Twig, seated in a corner of the room, busily engaged with a new box of toys his Aunt Margaret had sent him the day before. Suddenly he bethought himself of the fire, and soon had a beautifully long piece of paper ready. The next minute he was kneeling down before the fire; his chubby arm was pushed through the bars of the guard, and the paper between the bars of the grate. It soon took flame, and delighted, the little fellow forgot all his former promises, and ran through the open door straight across the passage into Georgie's room opposite, where he heard her moving, shouting at the top of his baby voice, "Deordie, Deordie, look here!"

At this moment a gust of wind from an open

window blew the flames towards his face. He dropped the paper, but one of his long curls had taken fire, and in an instant his head was in a blaze! One scream he gave, and rushed into Georgie's arms as she came out of her room to meet him. Without the slightest hesitation she snatched up the front of her dress (a thick serge one), and flinging it over him, endeavoured to extinguish the flames, at the same time pressing the unfortunate child tightly in her arms. He seemed stunned, for he uttered no cry, though his groans of pain were audible. His clothes did not seem to burn. Georgie raised the end of her dress from his face, gave a wild shriek, and thrust him from her. He fell to the floor. Georgie herself was in flames—her dress had taken fire! Her screams soon brought people to her aid; but the flames seemed almost to envelop her.

Nurse was the first to reach the room. She snatched up Twig, placed him in safety on the bed; and in less time than it takes to relate it, she and Mr. Merton between them dragged poor Georgie to the floor, and rolled her over and over in the hearth-rug, whilst Miss Acton frantically seized hold of the water-jug and threw its contents over her. The servants were at the door, keeping back the frightened children from entering the room.

"Send for the doctor at once," called out Mr. Merton.

"Say what for," added Miss Acton.

Away rushed Tom; and five minutes after a man was riding to the doctor's house as fast as the horse could carry him.

As soon as the flames had been put out, Georgie was lifted on to the bed by Twig's side; and the poor little boy, having recovered consciousness, mingled his moans and cries with hers. Nurse examined him very gently, and found that, though all his pretty curls were burned away, and his neck was badly scorched, still he was not burned so much as at first they had dreaded; his dress was unharmed. As for Georgie, she seemed to be in a most terrible condition; her clothes were entirely burned away in parts, and they feared to touch her till the doctor came. Nurse and Miss Acton undressed Twig; and cutting off the blackened remains of his hair, they covered his burns with oil and cotton-wool; whilst Mr. Merton bent over Georgie with an agonized countenance, unable to do aught to appease her sufferings. Once she opened her eyes, and gave him a faint smile, but groaned in anguish the next moment.

At last, after what seemed to the watchers hours

The rescue.

of time, the doctor arrived; and with him came in Mrs. Merton and Lily, who had been out for a drive, and had returned home just as Dr. Barton reached the house. Surprised to see him, and horrified when they heard the reason of his visit, together they hastened upstairs to Georgie's room. It was a sickening sight that met their eyes there. Little Twig, with his head and neck all bound up, lay sobbing on the bed, with Miss Acton and nurse bending over him; whilst on the opposite side lay Georgie—her face ghastly to behold, with closed eyes, uttering the most heart-rending moans, her clothes from her waist to her feet a blackened mass, and one hand holding her unhappy father's with an almost painful gripe.

It was a sight to bring sorrow to any mother's heart. Mr. Merton, fearing the shock would have been too much for her, would have hindered her from coming near enough to see the extent of the harm done. But the greatness of the shock seemed to give her strength; and she said, in a strangely calm, steady voice, "How did it happen?" No one could tell, for as yet no one had thought of inquiring.

Dr. Barton examined Twig first, and said nothing more could be done for him; nurse had acted quite rightly. The child was more scorched than burned,

(27)   10

and the shock had frightened him; so he was committed to nurse's special charge, who carried him off to his own little crib.   Miss Acton and Lily went to the school-room to see after the other children; and the room was cleared of all save Mr. and Mrs. Merton, whilst Dr. Barton devoted his attention to Georgie. She screamed when he attempted to touch her; but at last, after a short time, he was enabled, by using the greatest care, to remove some parts of the burned remains of her clothes, so as to see more clearly the extent of her injuries.   His face grew more and more serious, and Mr. and Mrs. Merton could gather no hope from it.   In some places the flesh seemed burned away to the bone.   He applied, with the utmost gentleness and the most tender touch, what remedies he could to allay the pain, and then withdrew from the room, motioning to Mr. Merton to follow him.

In the passage he placed his hand on his arm, and said, in answer to the questioning look in the father's face, "My friend, I fear you must prepare for the worst.   I can do nothing; she is in God's hands."

Mr. Merton staggered as if he had been shot, and, leaning against the wall, covered his face with his hands, and uttered a groan that seemed to come from the depths of his heart.   Dr. Barton did not disturb him for a few minutes. At length he roused himself, and uncovered his face. He seemed in those few minutes to have grown ten years older.

"Are you sure? are you certain?" he asked in a hollow voice. "Is there nothing more can be done?"

"Nothing beyond what I have already done; but if it would comfort you at all, telegraph for Dr. Eton, and I will stay here till he comes."

Dr. Eton was a celebrated medical man in a neighbouring town, and three or four hours at the very least must elapse before he could arrive. Nevertheless Mr. Merton seemed to snatch at the idea, and a man was soon riding off at full gallop with the telegram.

Dr. Barton and Mr. Merton now returned to the sick-room. Mrs. Merton was standing by the bed holding Georgie's hand in hers; it seemed to soothe the poor girl for some one to hold her hand. Lily was standing at the other side of the bed, endeavouring to pour a little wine down her throat. Her eyes were closed, and her face was white as the pillow it rested upon; whilst her pretty golden hair lay in disordered confusion, the only bright spot upon the bed. Her moans were still most pitiful to listen to; but she had not lost consciousness, for when her father and Dr. Barton entered the room she opened her eyes, looked at them, and then asked, in a faint voice, "How is Twig?"

"He is better now, my darling," said her father; whilst Dr. Barton added,—

"He is not so very much burned, and will soon be quite well, Miss Georgie. Is the pain very bad now?"

"Awful!" said the sufferer; and again her eyes closed.

Very sad and very wretched did the watchers feel as the time wore slowly by, unable as they were to do anything, and longing for the arrival of Dr. Eton. The shades of evening came gradually on. All sounds were hushed; every one moved about with muffled footsteps. The younger members of the family were sent by the doctor's orders early to bed, with the promise that they should be called should Georgie be taken worse.

Evening grew into night, and still Dr. Eton came not. Another telegram was sent. Mr. and Mrs. Merton and Dr. Barton watched by the bedside. Lily, in the next room, tried to comfort her eldest brother, who had been sent for, and upon whom the blow fell very heavily. Nurse took care of little Twig.

During the long hours of that dreadful night Georgie's reason left her, and she talked wildly and

strangely. "Twig, Twig," she would cry out, "the
fire will kill you! Oh, my sonnie! your sweet curls!
—Mother, mother, oh, I did try to put the fire out!—
I tell you, Harry Hamilton, you are not to go on that
rock, you young donkey, or you will break your
neck.—The sea is coming—oh, so quickly! And
such flames!—Father, don't be very angry; I never
will be naughty again.—And I may have the long-
eared rabbit for Con, mayn't I?—My ankle is better
now.—O Twig! I am glad you are up in the tree,
and not with me on the bull's back!—Oh, I cannot
hold on much longer! Save me! Oh, do, do
save me!"

Thus, through the stillness of the hours of darkness, did the poor child talk on, whilst the watchers
listened with breaking hearts. As dawn appeared
she grew a little more tranquil, and Dr. Barton managed to pour a soothing draught down her throat.
She became quieter and quieter; she did not move.
The old doctor bent over her and listened to her
breathing; it came gently and evenly. Georgie was
asleep.

Hour after hour slipped away, and still she slumbered on. Dr. Barton insisted upon Mrs. Merton,
who was well-nigh exhausted, lying down for a while.
She would not leave the room, so she lay on the floor

by the bedside with a pillow under her head, scarcely
able to realize where she was or what had happened.
It was all so sudden, this great trouble that had
come upon them, that it seemed impossible to be real.

It was not until the sun was shining brightly that
Georgie awoke from her deep sleep. She opened her
eyes and gazed around her.

"My darling, how do you feel now?" asked Mrs.
Merton tenderly, and at the same time kissing her
pale cheek.

"Very well, thank you, mother dear. But why
are you here, and Dr. Barton too? Have I been ill?"

Mrs. Merton turned away her head in mute agony
and her husband answered for her.

"Dear child, have you forgotten you were on fire?"

A shudder ran through Georgie's frame, and she
closed her eyes for a moment. When she opened
them again they seemed larger, and there was a
strange light in them as she said,—

"The pain is gone, father, so I had forgotten; but
there is something tells me I am never going to get
well again. Isn't it so? Don't be afraid to tell me,"
she pleaded.

"My child! my child!" was all the answer she received from her father, as he sat at the foot of her
bed with his hands over his face; but she thought

she read the truth in her mother's tear-stained countenance and Dr. Barton's sorrowful expression. The latter, however, who was in the act of feeling her pulse, said,—

"You are in God's hands, Miss Georgie, and if He wills it, you may recover even yet. There is just a chance."

"*Only* a chance!" repeated Georgie. "Well, I am not afraid to die. I know God will take care of me, so don't cry, mother dear; and, please, I would like to say 'Good-bye' to every one now. May they all come?"

"Oh! where is Dr. Eton? Why does not he come?" murmured Mr. Merton to himself, as he went at once to summon his other children. In a few minutes the entire family was assembled round Georgie's bed, and a strange gathering it was. Norman and Lily looked weary and worn with their night's watch. The younger ones were all as they had left their beds, with shawls and wraps thrown round them; for it was yet early in the morning, before their ordinary hour for rising. Alice's face was filled with awe, and she and Conrad were weeping bitterly; little Twig was enveloped in a blanket in nurse's arms; and Miss Acton had tight hold of Tom's hand, who seemed too much frightened to think or act for himself.

"Are they all here?" asked the sick girl.

"Yes, darling, every one."

"Please, father, would you say the Lord's Prayer and a prayer for me too, please?"

Mr. Merton knelt down; the others followed his example; and in trembling tones he repeated the prayer his child had asked for.

"Say one for me too; do, please, father dear!"

Obedient to this appeal, the unhappy man cried out from the bottom of his heart,—

"O God, my God, have pity! oh, have pity upon us, and spare my child! Father, into Thine hands I commend my darling. Hear me, I implore Thee, for Christ's sake. Amen."

Then he arose from his knees, and kissed Georgie passionately.

"Thank you, dear father.—And now, please, each one come and say 'Good-bye,' because I think I am dying, though I am very sorry to leave you all. I shall watch over you all from heaven, and I shall ask God to send His angels to see after you very often. —Norman, dear, will you kiss me good-bye?"

Round to the side of the bed came the tall youth, and, bending over Georgie, kissed her very lovingly, and said, in a hollow, broken voice,—

"Farewell, little sister! Heaven knows what we shall do without you."

Lily came next, and as she embraced her, she tried hard to speak, but without avail; so she in turn moved aside, to make room for Alice.

"You will forgive me, Allie, won't you, dear, all the times I have plagued you and tried to make you cross? I am so sorry now."

Alice cried out, "O Georgie, Georgie! it was my fault always! don't, don't talk like that."

Con came next, and very, very loving was the parting embrace between the twins. Those around could not hear all that Georgie whispered in his ear, but something about "Be a man," and "Take courage," was audible.

Con's answer was, "O Geo, my Geo! I never can live without you! What shall I do? what shall I do?"

Dr. Barton, seeing his grief was exhausting his patient, moved him gently aside; whilst Tom, who came next, shed not a tear, but kissed her affectionately. And when she said, "You will try and not get into scrapes when you have not got me to lead you into them, won't you, Tom, my boy?" he replied in a brave voice,—

"I would rather be in scrapes every day of my life than lose you, Georgie."

Nurse now brought Twig in her arms, and placed

him on the bed by Georgie's side. The little fellow was wide awake, and looked very strange with the bandages over his head. Georgie asked, turning her face to Dr. Barton, who from time to time made her swallow a tea-spoonful of wine and water,—

" He will get quite well, won't he ?"

" Oh yes, Miss Georgie ; he will be all right in a few weeks, with his curls beginning to grow again."

" I am so glad, though I don't suppose I shall be here to see them.—Twig, my sonnie, will you promise sister Geo never to play with fire any more ?"

" Yes, me will," answered Twig resolutely.

" Remember, sonnie, I shall see you from heaven if you do."

" Is you dooing to die, Deo ? Persons must be dead first before they can tlimb up to Dod in heaven."

" Yes, darling Twiggie ; I think I am dying. But kiss me, if you can without hurting your head—a sweet kiss."

Nurse held him up; for a moment his baby lips touched those of the dying girl, who then closed her eyes, and murmured in a faint voice,—

" Oh dear, I am so tired, and my legs are hurting me so badly !"

At these words, Dr. Barton hurriedly felt her pulse

again; and at the same minute a servant appeared to say Dr. Eton had arrived.

"Clear the room, and bring him up instantly!" said Dr. Barton, before any one else could answer.

He then made Georgie swallow a few drops of a powerful stimulant, and had just done so when Dr. Eton entered. Soon the two doctors were left alone with their patient, who now lay with closed eyes, apparently sleeping, but giving a little moan every now and then, as they touched her poor burned limbs. Then, after a short consultation in another room, the joyful news was given out that Georgie would not die, but live, though her recovery would be very slow; and, alas! for the rest of her life she would be a cripple.

CHAPTER XI.

DRESSING UP.

T is the morning of Christmas-Eve, a year afterwards. The children, except Georgie, are all assembled in the school-room; and, to judge from the eager expression of their faces and the animated way they are talking, something very entertaining is going on. They do not look much changed from what they were a twelvemonth before; though, of course, they are grown taller and older.

"It certainly would be most uncommonly jolly, Alice; there isn't a doubt of that," said Tom; "but do you think we ever could manage it without any one knowing?"

"Easily," said his sister; "there won't be the slightest difficulty about that, if you boys will only promise to do as we tell you. We must let nurse into the secret, though, for we are bound to have some one to help in the getting ready, and she will do that first-rate.—Twig, there's a pet, just run and ask nurse if she will come down here. Tell her we want her awfully for something extremely important; but mind, you are not to say what."

"Want nurse—tumthing ecthremely important— not say what," repeated Twig, who lisped as badly as ever; and then away flew the little messenger, re-appearing in a few minutes with nurse, who had certainly grown no thinner during the past year.

"Well now, Miss Alice, and what in the world do you want with me, that I am to be dragged down from my work in this fashion?"

"Now, nurse, don't be cross, there's a dear old soul, we—"

"None of your 'dear old souls' to me, if you please, Miss Alice."

"Well, then, nurse, there's a nice young girl, we—"

Again Alice was interrupted, this time by the fits of laughter called forth by her new mode of address.

"Will you stop, boys? I really can't speak for the row! Listen nurse: now, seriously, it really is something extremely important. You know to-day is Christmas-Eve, and we want to have a grand dressing-up to-night. Mother told me the Arm-strongs, and Mr. Hazlewood, and Aunt Margaret, are all coming to dinner; so we shall have lots of people

to look at us. Last Christmas, you know, we had
no fun,—we couldn't without Georgie; so this year
we want to have something awfully swell to make
up. Will you promise to help us, nurse, and not to
tell our secret? Do, please, say 'Yes!'"

"Humph! I suppose I must. But, quick now,
tell me what it is you want me to do, Miss
Alice."

Just then stump, stump was heard outside, and
with one accord they all flew to open the door and
admit Georgie and her crutch. It was the same
Georgie as of old, taller and thinner; her hair cut
short, but forming little curls all over her head; her
eyes honest and true as ever, though, if you watched
her closely, every now and then you would perceive
that a gleam of sadness would chase the sunshine from
them; and there were about her face certain signs
of suffering almost hidden now by her bonny smile
—yes, the same smile you used to notice in former
days, but gentler and sweeter.

"That's right, dear Geo," said Con; "I thought
you would keep your promise and come."

"I have had an awful bother to persuade mother
to let me, though, because she declared I should be
doing too much.—Here, Tom, old boy, take my crutch,
and give me your shoulder over to the sofa. If I

deposit myself there, mother will be quite satisfied; don't you think so, nurse?"

"If you stay there, Miss Georgie, she will be, of course; but you had much better have stayed downstairs out of harm's way."

"Now, nurse, I'll call you a cross-old-soul-nasty-young-girl if you try to get Geo away," said Tom. "Why shouldn't she have a bit of fun as well as the rest of us, I should like to know?—You can help in a quiet way; can't you, Geo dear?"

"Of course I can; and I am going to, too."

"Well, well, child; all I mean is, don't go and tire yourself—that's all—or you won't get any fun to-night.—Now, Miss Alice, what do you want me to do?"

"Oh, heaps of things, nurse. We are going to bring in the Yule-log, and dress up like people used to at Christmas in olden times. Oh, it will be splendid! I am to be a dragon; Con, a hobby-horse; Tom, a clown; and, only fancy, nurse, Twig is to be Father Christmas! We are going to drag him into the room seated on that old piece of tree down by the arbour; that's to be the Yule-log."

"Gracious me!" ejaculated nurse. "My baby boy to be Father Christmas! Well, to be sure; and what next, I should like to know?"

"Oh, nothing else; only we want you to help us to get ready; all our dresses, I mean. You see it is past eleven o'clock now, and there are lots of things to be done."

"I shall be able to help Alice a good bit, nurse; but we want you as well," put in Georgie.

"I tell you what it is, Miss Alice; you had better come straight up to the nursery, and do the things there. I'll just go up and put away my work, and I shall be ready to do anything you like.—As for you, Miss Georgie dear, I think you will find it livelier like up there too; so, if you come up, I will get your own couch brought up, and then you can rest as much as you like."

"You are a dear, good-natured old—I beg your pardon; I mean young woman! We will be up in a few minutes," said Alice.

Off went nurse; and then Alice set Conrad to teach Twig some lines he would have to repeat, which said lines she had composed herself. The whole afternoon Alice and Georgie never stirred from the nursery; and as the boys were up there also most of the time, with the door fast locked, the elder members of the family could not help being suspicious that some pleasant surprise was in store for them, and wisely refrained from making inquiries.

It must be confessed, though, that when the house-maid came to Mrs. Merton with a message from Alice, asking if she would lend her a small sofa-cushion, and her scarlet flannel dressing-gown, she was rather perplexed to know what could possibly be in preparation. Her curiosity was raised to a still higher pitch when, quarter of an hour later, the servant reappeared to request the loan of three white skin mats from the drawing-room.

What fun the children had in making their dresses can well be imagined. They had to work hard, though, to get them ready. Poor Alice was sorely puzzled about her own disguise, especially the tail; but here Georgie came to the rescue, and insisted that she could manage it beautifully, if nurse would only rummage out some old green lining that she knew was in existence somewhere or other. It was found at last; and then she set to work with a will, determined to succeed. Con was nearly the same height as Alice now, so she made him serve as her block; and many a laugh there was at the wry faces he made at the number of times he had to attire himself in the strange garment. Alice was charmed with the effect of it when finished; and at last every-thing was in readiness, and the boys thoroughly in-structed in what they had to do.

It was about five o'clock when the preparations were announced to be complete; and then, following nurse's advice, the whole party, except, of course, Georgie, betook themselves down to the hall, there to indulge in a good game of battledore and shuttle-cock. Norman and Lily, attracted by their merry shouts, soon joined them, very wisely not thinking that, because they were grown up, they were too old to enjoy a game with their younger sister and brothers. They played till the school-room bell rang for tea, and by then it was nearly time for Norman and Lily to depart to dress for dinner.

Meanwhile Georgie had had a long nap, and was feeling quite fresh and rested. Tea being over, and nurse having ascertained that the guests had arrived, and that every one was safely out of the way in at dinner, she and Alice descended to the drawing-room and moved aside some of the furniture, so as to leave a large clear space. At last dinner, as well as tea, was over; and in the drawing-room, where Georgie was comfortably sitting in an arm-chair, looking very pretty in her white dress and blue ribbons, with a bright, happy look upon her face, quite a large party was assembled. All were so busily engaged in talking that no one had noticed the journeys that had been taken by various chairs and tables, except Mrs.

Merton, who judiciously held her tongue. Presently their conversation was interrupted by the loud ringing of a bell; and then the door was flung wide open, and the butler, entering, said that he had been ordered by Father Christmas to request the company to be seated, as he was about to pay them a visit. This command was immediately obeyed, and every one was on the tiptoe of expectation, whilst the servants came in and arranged themselves down one side of the room. The bell then sounded again, and distant hurrahs were heard. In a few seconds a small figure appeared dressed as a clown, in a suit of white glazed calico, with one arm red and the other blue, and his stockings contrasting in like manner. Round his throat was a huge paper ruff; his face was painted white, with peculiar red spots on it; and on his head was a dunce's cap, from the sides of which projected two donkey's ears. His entrance was hailed with shrieks of laughter, which, however, did not abash him in the slightest degree, for he merely made profound bows right and left; and at last, when he seemed to consider that they had laughed at him sufficiently, he opened his bright red lips and shrieked out "Silence!" at the top of his voice. Silence ensued.

" Ladies and gentlemen,—Father Christmas is com-

ing to see you. Make room, I say—make room!"
So saying, he strutted round the open space that
nurse and Alice had cleared out during dinner, ringing a bell and brandishing a long white wand. A
great noise as of stamping and kicking was now
heard approaching, and then a green dragon appeared
in sight, and a hobby-horse, both of which seemed to
be dragging something into the room. Then a broken
piece of the trunk of a tree was seen, on the top of
which a most charming little Father Christmas was
seated, round whom the dragon and the hobby-horse
performed the most marvellous dance. The hobby-
horse was formed out of pink calico, and possessed
the biggest eyes and the longest mane that can possibly be imagined. He snorted and kicked and
pranced about in the most wonderful manner. The
green dragon was no less active, and wriggled about
its tail to such an extent that a sound came forth
strangely similar to that produced by a lot of buttons
put into a tin box. Its body was of a brilliant green
hue, ornamented with sundry leopard-like spots of
white paint; whilst its head was in shape something
between a fish and a bird, and out of its mouth hung
a huge red flannel tongue, which made its large white
card-board teeth look most formidable. The clown
joined in the dance, and a most extraordinary affair

it certainly was, quite unlike any other seen before
or since.   Presently, having given utterance to a
prodigious roar, the dragon threw itself at full length
on the floor, and remained perfectly still, except its
tail, which kept moving up and down at intervals.
The hobby-horse also reposed himself; and then the
clown sprang up upon the Yule-log behind Father
Christmas, and made most fearful grimaces.   Father
Christmas, however, was not to be disturbed, and
treated him with the utmost indifference.   The old
man was arrayed in a magnificent scarlet gown,
which hung in heavy folds round his uncommonly
stout figure; his hair was snow-white, and fell over
his shoulders in flowing locks; his beard reached
down to his waist.   For the information of any of
our readers who may be of a curious turn of mind,
we will mention that both hair and beard were com
posed of the mats borrowed that afternoon.   His
head was crowned with a wreath of holly; he had
thick white shaggy eye-brows, big spectacles, and a
monstrous red nose, that Alice had made out of paste,
and painted with vermilion.   His feet were encased
in Mr. Merton's Wellington boots; his hands were
covered by huge white gloves, the fingers of which
were stuffed with paper.   After a few minutes, the
clown assisted him to stand upright, for he was some

what feeble in his movements; and then, advancing
in front of him, bowed politely to the audience, and
said,—

"Ladies and gentlemen, let me present Father
Christmas to you."

A tremendous clapping of hands from all present
proved what a welcome guest the old man was. And
then he, lifting one hand, in which was a bunch of
mistletoe, high up, so that all might see it, said,—

> " To see you all I've tum,
>   'Tis long since I've been here;
> A year away has wun,
>   Still Kismas brings dood cheer.
> Ladies, I love you well,
>   Here is the mithletoe "—

" O Alice! my nose is off!"

This most extraordinary ending to Father Christmas's address was really too much for the audience.
Shriek succeeded shriek of laughter; and when the
old man carefully placed his huge foot on the back
of the prostrate dragon, and made vain efforts to pick
up his nose with his enormous fingers, it almost
seemed as if the spectators were beside themselves,
so great was their merriment. However, in the end,
the clown rescued the unfortunate nose, and then
Father Christmas waddled across the room to Mrs.
Merton, and said in the most supplicating tone,—

" Please, mother, will you 'tick it on for me?"

The performance being now over, the actors came amongst the company to be admired, and Alice received immense praise for the capital way in which she had got up the disguises, and, in fact, the whole affair. She, however, declared that it all originated with Georgie, and that she herself deserved no praise; whilst Georgie was equally sure that it was all Alice's doing. Any way, the evening was pronounced a perfect success, and no one felt willing to bring it to an end. But bed-time came at last, and thither departed every one except Mr. and Mrs. Merton, who usually sat up an hour or two later than the rest of the family.

CHAPTER XII.

GOOD-NIGHT.

THAT night the last thing, when Mrs. Merton was going the round of the children's rooms, she was surprised to find that Georgie was still awake.

"What is it darling? how is it you are not asleep? I am afraid you must be over-tired."

"No, I am not, mother dear; I was only thinking. I wish, oh, I do wish sometimes that I could just have my leg well, if only for an hour, just to do everything for a little time like I used to. I know 'tis wicked, mother, to be so discontented; but indeed, I never knew how dearly I loved being able to get about till I got lame."

"I know it is, it must be, a heavy trial for you, my own precious child, and I would I could do anything to make it lighter."

"Never mind, mother darling, it is all right as it is, and I ought not to grumble. Why, only fancy, if

It had been one of the boys instead of me. How much more horrid it would have been for either of them to have to keep quiet. 'Tisn't half so bad for me, because I am only a girl. Good-night, mother. I mean this Christmas to be an uncommonly happy one, though I am what that sweet Twig calls 'a cwipple.'"

Just then a clock sounded the hour of twelve.

"May your Christmas be happier each year, my darling," said Mrs. Merton, kissing her tenderly, "and may God bless you and make you His own child."

"What should I do without her?" thought Mrs. Merton to herself, as she wended her way to the night nursery. "I think I love her more and more every day. With all her faults she is the good angel of our house. But what's the matter?" she said aloud, addressing nurse, who was leaning over Twig, who was sitting up in bed, looking flushed and excited; "is anything wrong?"

"He woke up dreaming, ma'am; that's all."

"What is it, my pet?" asked Mrs. Merton anxiously. "What have you been dreaming about? Tell mother."

"Oh, such a tream, mother, such a lovely tream! I thought Deo had dorne out for a walk, and that she had met a bootiful white angel, who said, 'tause it was Kismas, he would show her where was Jacob's ladder, for her to det up quickly to heaven. And Deo was so glad, and so happy, and she and her old cutch began to doo up—up and up; and den all of a tudden Deo saw me at the bottom of the drate long ladder, so she tame down, though it hurt her poor leg awfly much, and tissed me such a lot, and talled herself a nasty, telfish girl, 'tause she had fordotten her sonnie; and den she made me doo up in front ot her; and went so high up—higher and higher, and higher—till we were just dooing to 'tep into heaven frough a 'plendid dold date, and den I woke. Dat's all my tream. Does you like it, mother dear?" asked Twig breathlessly, for he had been talking as fast as his tongue would go.

"Yes, darling, very much. It was very kind of sister Georgie to come back for you. Wasn't it dear?"

"Oh yes, mother; but Deo is always dood to me. Tuck me up comfy, mother. I wants to doo to tleep now, 'tause I'm tired. Dear Deo! I do love her. Dood-night, mother."

Mrs. Merton seated herself in a chair by his little bed, prepared to watch till he should once more fall asleep. The little fellow lay quite still for several minutes with his eyes fast shut. Suddenly he opened them, and looking straight up at his mother, who was leaning over him, he said, very seriously,—

"Mother, don't you t'ink Dod must be a very nice tind dentleman, to ask us all up to His lubly house in Heaven? I wish—I do wish dere was a train dooing up dere. I weally t'inks I s'all ask Him to make one, when I say my p'ayers in the morning. He could make one, couldn't He, mother?"

"Yes, Twiggie; God can do everything. But try to sleep now, there's a darling."

At last he slumbered; but as his mother pressed a parting kiss on his sweet face the rosy lips murmured, "Dear Deo!" And with a tear in her eye, but joy in her heart, Mrs. Merton left him.

THE END.

PRINTED IN GREAT BRITAIN AT
THE PRESS OF THE PUBLISHERS

NELSON'S STORIES FOR BOYS, GIRLS, AND CHILDREN.

Cloth, 1s. 9d. net.

FOR BOYS.

SALE'S SHARPSHOOTERS.	Harold Avery.
HIGHWAY PIRATES.	Harold Avery.
PRESTER JOHN.	John Buchan.
HOW WE BAFFLED THE GERMANS.	Eric Wood.
DOING HIS BIT.	Tom Bevan.
SECRET SERVICE SUBMARINE.	Guy Thorne.
HIGHWAY DUST.	G. G. Sellick.
MOBSLEY'S MOHICANS.	Harold Avery.
DIAMOND ROCK.	J. Macdonald Oxley.
THE FELLOW WHO WON.	Andrew Home.

FOR GIRLS.

GIRLS OF CROMER HALL.	Raymond Jacberns.
OLIVE ROSCOE.	E. Everett-Green.
DORIS HAMLYN.	R. O. Chester.
KITTY TRENIRE.	Mabel Quiller-Couch.
BOSOM FRIENDS.	Angela Brazil.
WASTE CASTLE.	W. M. Letts.
LITTLE WOMEN.	Louisa M. Alcott.
A PAIR OF RED POLLS.	Mabel Quiller-Couch.
THE LITTLE HEIRESS.	Margaret B. Clarke.
GLADYS OR GWENYTH.	E. Everett-Green.

FOR CHILDREN.

THE STORY OF HEATHER.	May Wynne.
NELLIE O'NEILL.	Agnes C. Maitland.
SQUIB AND HIS FRIENDS.	E. Everett-Green.
SIX DEVONSHIRE DUMPLINGS.	Margaret Batchelor.
THE GREEN TOBY JUG.	Mrs. Edwin Hohler.
TELL ME SOME MORE.	Mary Few.
WHEN MOTHER WAS IN INDIA.	Ursula Temple.
HUMPTY DUMPTY AND THE PRINCESS.	Lilian Timpson.
GOLDEN FAIRY TALES.	
THE TWINS AND SALLY.	E. L. Haverfield.

T. NELSON & SONS, LTD., PUBLISHERS.

NELSON'S NOVELS.

Cloth. 2s. net.

DESERT GOLD.	Zane Grey.
THE LIGHT OF WESTERN STARS.	Zane Grey.
THE HERITAGE OF THE DESERT.	Zane Grey.
RIDERS OF THE PURPLE SAGE.	Zane Grey.
THE LONE STAR RANGER.	Zane Grey.
THE RAINBOW TRAIL.	Zane Grey.
THE BORDER LEGION.	Zane Grey.
WILDFIRE.	Zane Grey.
THE GOLDEN KINGDOM.	Andrew Balfour.
THE RANGE DWELLERS.	B. M. Bower.
CHIP, OF THE FLYING U.	B. M. Bower.
THE HAPPY FAMILY.	B. M. Bower.
THE LONESOME TRAIL.	B. M. Bower.
THE SOWERS.	H. Seton Merriman.
THE LURE OF THE DIM TRAILS.	B. M. Bower.
HER PRAIRIE KNIGHT.	B. M. Bower.
THE LONG SHADOW.	B. M. Bower.
THE FLYING U RANCH.	B. M. Bower.